Hissy Fit

Book 1 of The Southern Gentleman Series

By

Lani Lynn Vale

Lani Lynn Vale

ISBN- 9781796897005

Dedication

This story was inspired by my husband. A long time ago, when we met, it was during football season. You can thank him for what you're about to read! <3

Acknowledgements

Quinn Biddle- Model

Golden Czermak- Photographer

Ellie McLove- My Brother's Editor & Ink It Out Editing

Cover Me Darling, LLC

My mom- Thank you for reading this book eight million two hundred times.

Diane, Kendra, Kathy, Mindy, Barbara & Amanda—I don't know what I would do without y'all. Thank you, my lovely betas, for loving my books as much as I do.

Hissy Fit

CONTENTS

Hissy Fit

Lani Lynn Vale

CHAPTER 1

Women my age are supposed to be able to look
suave and sophisticated while walking in heels.
Me? I manage to trip over thin air.

-Raleigh's inner thoughts

Raleigh

If there was one thing in this world that I never wanted to do, it was embarrassing myself in front of *him*.

Ezra McDuff, the town bad boy, high school football *and* baseball coach. was everything I was not.

Suave. Cool. Coordinated.

Then there was me.

My name conjured fear in the hearts of all residents of Gun Barrel, Texas.

Why, you ask, would an innocent woman like me, the woman that every single kid in town screamed a hello to because she was the 'best teacher ever,' strike that kind of fear?

That'd be because I, Raleigh Jolie Crusie, was the clumsiest person in four counties.

And normally when I went down, I took people with me.

For instance, moments before, I'd been walking.

Sure, I'd been looking down at my phone because I was reading…but that's beside the point.

Who the hell put clearance Christmas shit in the middle of a godforsaken aisle?

Target, that's who.

There I was, walking and minding my own business while I caught up on my latest read, and the next thing that I know, I ran into a large box of wrapping paper.

And when I say 'large,' I mean *large*.

There wasn't just one box, either.

There were multiple boxes.

Fifteen, in fact.

But, I'd walked past four such boxes before I'd tripped on thin air—like always—and took a header to the left.

I managed to cradle my phone to my chest and tuck and roll, but that also made me into a human bowling ball.

I took down not one, not two, not nine, but eleven boxes jam-packed with wrapping paper.

And every last roll of wrapping paper fell out of the boxes and started rolling in every which direction.

Meaning that not only did it get me, but it got four other people in the process.

Jennifer Marie, the beauty consultant at Ulta that was here getting a coffee. Brian McAdams, the young sales clerk that I'd taught three years ago and was now an assistant manager in this fine establishment. Larry Conway, the electrician. And finally, Ezra *freakin'* McDuff.

Though, Ezra didn't exactly go down like the rest of the people did.

He only tripped on one and dropped what looked like an armful of undershirts and underwear.

Boxer briefs.

Boxer briefs that landed directly next to my face.

But apparently, clothing hadn't been the only thing Ezra had been holding.

He was holding a box of condoms, too.

Why do I know that particular detail?

Because the box smacked me in the face, and, like the loser my nose was, it started to bleed.

He made me bleed by dropping a box of condoms. On. My. Nose.

Dear sweet baby Jesus on a cracker.

I grumbled and held onto my nose as I felt the blood start to pour out.

The only good thing I could say about it was that it was one of those value sized packs, not just the small ones that had like twelve condoms in it...not that I would know. I'd never bought condoms before, so who knew? Maybe the value size was really the smaller package.

The closest I'd ever gotten to the condoms was when I was buying tampons, and even then, they were still half an aisle away from the offending pieces of latex.

I wailed and rolled onto my hands and knees.

Instead of waiting around for cleanup, and knowing what a bleeder I was, I started to make a mad dash toward the bathroom where I could find something to hold over my nose.

The first thing I came to once I was inside were the paper towels.

I moaned as I covered my nose with a handful of towels, cursing the stupid machine when it only spit out a small square of paper at a time.

God.

Anybody. Anybody in the freakin' world could've hit me in the nose with those condoms, and I would've been okay. Anybody but Ezra McDuff.

Shit.

Shit. Shit. *Shit.*

I panted into the paper and rested my head against the cool, white-tiled wall beside the dispenser.

Then I counted to one hundred, hoping that would help.

It didn't.

But what it did do was give my nose enough time to stop bleeding.

I reached for my phone, thinking now would be a perfect time to call my best friend, Camryn, and tell her about my humiliation.

But…it wasn't there.

I closed my eyes and realized what had happened.

When those condoms had hit me in the face, I'd dropped my phone to immediately raise my hands to my nose. And in doing so, had left my phone wherever it happened to be when my hand had discarded it.

Garnering the courage, I walked to the door and pushed.

When I opened the door, bloody paper towel still in my hand in case it started to bleed again, it was to find the best backside in Gun Barrel, Texas blocking the door.

"Uhhh," I hesitated. "'Scuse me."

Ezra turned around, saw my face, and blanched.

"Are you okay?"

He was looking at me like he'd never seen me before.

To be perfectly honest, he probably hadn't.

I wasn't exactly in Ezra McDuff's social circle.

I was more like that quiet girl in the corner at a party, while Ezra was the town hero and star quarterback all rolled into one.

The sad thing was, we worked at the same damn place. We probably passed each other in the halls half a dozen times every school day, if not more.

He was also staring right at me, and I was finding it hard to breathe.

I'd dreamed of this day so many times.

So. Many. Times.

In high school I used to sit behind him, studying his every move.

When I'd been a junior, and he'd been a senior, we had our first class together.

My last name started with a C, and his with an M. But, since he couldn't sit in the back thanks to some rule that the coach of the football team at the time had made, he'd had to move to the front, and I'd been pushed back a chair.

And, by doing so, I'd gotten to see his every single feature for an entire year.

Which had been how my infatuation with the man had begun.

At first, it'd only been my appreciation of his body.

He was six-foot-four, muscled, and strapping.

He was also funny, intelligent, and sweet.

He was a caregiver. He was a nurturer. And he also had no clue that I was alive, even then.

Now, he'd grown up quite a bit from that boy that I used to obsess over, but he was still no less captivating.

Today, he was in a simple pair of jeans—covered in dirt and grime from whatever he was doing—probably working on his old truck that he got in high school, and still drove on Sundays to this day.

His white t-shirt was stained, too.

And he had grease on his cheekbone.

His dirty blond hair was longer than normal, and some of it fell into his eyes. Those eyes that were a mix between a golden honey and a seafoam green.

At times, I wasn't able to tell which color was more prevalent, but I'd decided long ago that it was dependent on the color of shirt he was wearing at the time.

I swallowed when I got a load of the newest tattoo that peeked out from under his shirt sleeve.

It looked like a sugar skull, but honestly, I wasn't really sure without actually pulling his shirt sleeve up and looking. And that was creepy. I tried not to be creepy.

"Ma'am?"

I gritted my teeth.

He didn't even know who I was, but I could tell that I was familiar to him, at least somewhat.

He was studying me like he was trying to place how he knew me.

How about school from kindergarten up to my junior year. He had been two years older than me, and since the town of Gun Barrel was so small, the bus route had kids that ranged from kindergarten all the way up to seniors in high school. How about college? I knew Oklahoma State is a big campus, but he never saw me there even once? How about *work?* He never noticed me at all?

Dammit!

"I'm fine," I lied.

In all honesty, I was thoroughly embarrassed.

I was also sick at heart.

I had this idea in my mind that maybe I wasn't quite as invisible as I always felt like I was at times.

Apparently, if the football coach, who knew *everybody* didn't even know me, then I was a lost cause.

I smiled.

He winced.

That's because the movement forced the clot that had stopped the bleeding in my nose to break loose.

Blood trickled down my face.

And I decided now was the time to go.

That was when I looked down.

At my phone. In his hand.

He was holding it out to me.

I took it with shaking fingers as I placed the towel back to my face.

Then, to add insult to injury, I looked down to find my phone not only open but the book I'd been immersed in reading still up.

My cheeks flamed.

There was no way, with him holding it like he had been, that he hadn't scanned what it was that was on the screen.

None.

And what it was, was my latest book club read, a BDSM romance that had immediately grabbed my attention. Then kept it.

Oh. *Shit.*

"Thank you," I murmured, my face likely matching the blood that was probably staining my skin.

Then, I took my bloody towel, my phone, and hightailed it straight out of Target before I could do anything else stupid.

I also pretended that he didn't see me hit the door on the way out.

Because then I might've just crawled into a hole and died.

***

"This isn't the first time I've ever heard of someone getting a black eye from something pertaining to Ezra McDuff's dick," Camryn supplied.

I flipped her off.

"Go fuck yourself," I grumbled. "Is it really that bad?"

She winced. "It's not…good."

With my pale complexion, paired with my inky black hair…I didn't doubt that it was more than obvious that I not only had one shiner, but two.

From a box of condoms.

How does that even happen?

But I shouldn't be surprised. Bad things happened to Raleigh Jolie Crusie. Always had. Always would.

CHAPTER 2

I'm a ray of fucking sunshine.

-Coffee Cup

Ezra

Four hours earlier

"I'm going to be late," I said into my phone. "I have to run by the store and get somebody something."

That somebody was my sister's teenage son, Johnson. Johnson was a sixteen-year-old boy, who was on the verge of doing things that his mother would rather not think about. That being in the form of sex with his girlfriend.

How did I know this?

Because I saw them in the park last night, making out in his truck when he should've been at home asleep.

Now, I felt obligated to run by the store and buy him a box of condoms just to make sure he had them in case he needed them.

I wasn't sure if he did or not, but I'd rather be safe than sorry.

Or a great uncle.

That would suck.

"Okay," Cady, my sister, said. "But would you mind picking me up some wrapping paper? It's seventy-five percent off, and I haven't had a chance to go up there yet. There's no doubt that it'll be sold out by the time I get off at five."

I rolled my eyes.

That was the last damn thing I wanted to do, get fucking wrapping paper, but I'd do it for her.

I loved my sister, after all.

And she did make sure that I had food every single night.

We lived together—kind of.

She lived in the main house, and I was in what was now known as the 'brother suite' and not the mother-in-law suite.

I had my own kitchen and my own entrance, but I could also enter their living space, as they could access mine. Not that either one of us did that unless it was dinner time—or it was an emergency.

But there hadn't been one of those since my niece, Moira, had decided to make her entrance into this world a whole four weeks early while Cady's husband had been out of town working on the pipeline.

Now Grady was home more, well, if you called two weeks on, two weeks off home more, and they didn't have much need for me.

Me? I needed them, though. At least if I didn't want to eat out every single night of the week.

"Will do," I verbalized. "Let me know if you need anything else."

She gave an affirmative sound, and then hung up, losing track of what she was doing when her youngest son, Colton, asked her a question.

Colton was autistic, and after struggling in school for three years, they decided that he needed a different school that would work better for him. That school was out two more days, meaning her other two had already started while Colton was at home with my mom.

My mind was on Colton, so I wasn't paying as much attention when I opened the door, but I didn't miss the white streak of blond hair run past me as I tried to walk through it.

Frowning, I turned to see a little boy, about three or four years old, sprint toward the parking lot, and every single protective instinct inside of me started to take flight.

I ran after the boy and caught him before he could get past the stupid big red balls that lined the front walk.

I turned and hefted him up on my hip just as the mother came running out.

She took him from me, gave him a stern glare, and walked back inside without a word.

I stood there, stunned.

A thank you would've at least been nice!

Glaring at the woman's back as I followed her inside, I made my way to the men's section. While I was here, I might as well get the underwear and undershirts I'd been avoiding getting seeing as I fuckin' hated Target.

I couldn't walk into the damn store without running into someone I knew, and honestly, I was tired.

The football season had been a long one, and I hadn't gotten a chance to take a deep breath before I was forced to dive into baseball season. I had exactly two weeks before it was time to switch gears, and I wanted to take that time to recoup.

Going into Target would mean I'd have to talk to someone, I knew it.

Yet, my nephew's health was more important than my privacy, so I trudged into the store and headed straight for the underwear.

After finding the cheapest pack—I was a coach, not a millionaire—I snatched up a value-sized pack of white undershirts, and then made my way to the condom aisle. Once there, I snatched up the generic brand of condoms that was also the cheapest and made my way to the front of the store.

Lucky for me, they now had that self-checkout, otherwise I would never consider buying condoms in this town.

Hiding the offending box between the underwear and the shirts, I made my way to the middle of the store, spotting the wrapping paper in the middle of the aisle near the checkout.

A little kid darted out in front of me—the same one from earlier—and caused me to growl in frustration.

How hard was it to watch your kid? It was more than obvious that this one was trying extremely hard to be obstinate, and his mother was doing nothing to ensure that he was contained.

When the kid grabbed a box of Little Debbies off the shelf and started helping himself to the contents of the box, I just shook my head and went around him.

But, while my attention was occupied elsewhere, I hadn't been paying attention to what was in front of me.

One second, I was walking, and the next I nearly maimed myself on a roll of wrapping paper that'd slid under my foot.

Seconds later, about two hundred other rolls joined the first, taking four people down in its wake. A woman with her coffee, an employee in a red shirt that I thought I'd coached at one point in time a few years ago, the town electrician and a young woman with inky black hair and a banging body.

Unfortunately, the woman with the banging body got to be on the receiving end of my belongings, taking the box of condoms straight to the face, the pair of value-sized shirts acting like a hammer as it followed the box down.

Blood instantly spurted, and the woman rolled to her feet and made a mad dash to the bathroom, trailing blood behind her.

I stood there, stunned for about thirty seconds before all hell broke loose.

"Goddamn that woman," the employee said as he dragged himself up off the ground. "If there was a way to ban a person, I'd do it with her. I swear, every single time she comes in here, something happens."

I looked at the kid with a raised eyebrow. "Seems to me that you're being a little bitch."

I was a football coach—being nice wasn't really in my genetic makeup.

The kid sputtered, "Coach! You can't say that in here! Think of the kids!"

The one and only kid that I could still see, working on his second Little Debbie, had probably heard worse. His mother seemed like the type to let the television babysit him—and not censor what he watched.

I looked back at the employee, shook my head, and then took a step in the direction of where the woman had run, feeling a sense of urgency. I needed to know that she was okay.

I didn't know why, but I felt it, so I was going with my gut.

I kicked something when I took a step, and saw a phone amongst the blood, knowing instantly that it belonged to the woman.

Bending over, I picked it up and glanced at the lit screen.

Words, likely from an e-book, scrolled across the screen, but I didn't glance at them until I was leaning against the wall waiting for the woman to come out.

When I did, my heart skipped a beat.

He bent her over, trailing the blunt head of his cock down her spine, painting her back with his pre-cum.

My belly clenched, and I suddenly felt a different urgency take me.

Not willing to actually change the page, I read the screen over and over again, waiting for the woman to come out of the bathroom.

And when she did, I'd practically memorized the words.

Then I felt something tap me in the backside, causing me to turn.

"Excuse me," a husky, feminine voice said from behind me.

"Are you okay?" I blurted, seeing her blood-filled towel in her hand.

She nodded, but I didn't hear the words that came out of her mouth when she replied, because I was too focused on her face.

I felt terrible for hurting her, even if it was by accident.

"Ma'am?"

Then her eyes glanced down at the phone in my hand, and her face turned eight shades of red.

I had to fight not to smile.

I let the phone go when she reached for it.

"Thank you," she murmured.

Then, she turned, skirted around me, and started running for the door.

When the doors didn't open fast enough for her forward progress, she ran into one of them, and I had to hold in the burst of laughter that threatened to slip free.

That woman was a hot mess.

And I wanted to know more about her. Now.

CHAPTER 3

I'm a virgin.

(This isn't an old shirt)

-T-shirt

Raleigh

"What do you mean you want me to teach the sex-ed class this year?" I asked, appalled at the mere thought of having to have that discussion with teenagers when I hadn't even experienced the act myself.

The horror must've been evident on my face because Mrs. Sherpa hurried to explain.

"Normally this is handled by the coaches," Mrs. Sherpa explained. "But with the football team entering state finals last season, Coach McDuff had to roll straight from football to baseball. He doesn't have time to teach the health class." She exhaled. "And, you're the only one with an opening for the time period that health class would normally take place."

I didn't know what to say to that.

I mean, sure, that was the case with 'Coach McDuff.' The Gun Barrel Devil Dogs did, in fact, make it to state—and won.

The mere mention of 'Coach McDuff'—also known as Ezra Doran McDuff, sexy coach in my head—had my heart rate accelerating.

But…sex-ed.

I didn't do sex.

I didn't have sex.

I didn't know about sex.

I didn't even think about sex—okay, that last one is a lie. I thought about sex…with Ezra. I didn't think about sex with anyone else, though.

That, and I read about it. But reading about it and doing it were two entirely different things.

"W-what age group are we talking here?" I asked, hoping that it was with a bunch of immature ninth graders.

"Mainly, it'd be the junior and senior level. Grades ten and nine can move down to take health at the junior high, or we can put them off until next year due to availability. But the seniors don't have the choice to put it off. So, it'll be one class, with about thirty students in it."

That made me want to vomit.

I worked with the ninth graders because they were still too young to have attitudes, and they weren't so big that they could overpower me if they got pissed off. The upperclass boys—let's just say that if they wanted to, they could take me down in a heartbeat.

Just the idea of all those big football players in a class of mine made me nauseous.

I knew, logically, that they weren't going to do anything.

But thanks to my first and only foray into senior level classes when I was a student teacher—I'd quickly realized that senior classes weren't where I wanted to be.

But that was thanks to a certain senior, that was now a convict, in a maximum-security prison.

At the time, he'd only been a stupid seventeen, almost eighteen-year-old kid, that thought he'd be able to obtain an A by sexing up the student teacher. When I'd informed him that I was uninterested, he'd taken it as a personal affront, and had made it his mission in life to make my life hell.

Shortly after the end of the year, Cramer Winters, my personal stalker, failed his Algebra class. When he'd received his grade, he'd come to the office to complain to the teacher. Only, the teacher hadn't been there. I had.

And he'd sexually assaulted me—though he'd not gotten as far as he'd been intending.

Luckily, the actual teacher had walked in right about the time that Cramer had been about to penetrate me.

I'd been unconscious and bloody, unaware of the horror that the teacher had saved me from until much later on that day.

The bad thing was that another student had seen him assaulting me and hadn't done a thing about it.

That left a deep-seated fear in me when it came to the elder students that should've helped and didn't.

It'd taken everything I had to continue with my teaching degree. Then, when I'd tried to find a job with the younger age group, I'd hit hurdle after hurdle, until finally, I'd found a job working with the younger generation of high schoolers.

It was a good fit for me.

"I don't know…"

"Listen, Ms. Crusie. I'm going to be honest with you here. You're already one of the newest teachers here, that means that most of the other teachers have seniority. You're the most qualified. Either you take it, or we'll find someone new that can. Coach McDuff is willing to give you all of his materials and sit in on the first few classes to help smooth the transition over," Mrs. Sherpa was saying. "I know that you're nervous with teaching the upper levels due to your previous...problems. But he promises that it'll be okay. They're good kids, and most of them are his ball players. He can ensure that they stay in line."

She didn't have to say the words. I knew what she meant.

Either I did what I was being asked to do, or I would be fired, and someone else would be hired that could just as easily do my job and teach the sex-ed class.

"Fine," I said, my voice shaky. "When do you want me to start?"

She looked at her watch. "Now."

***

I arrived in the senior hallway and tried not to jump at the sound of lockers slamming, boisterous laughter, and the yells and shouts of the seniors all around me.

Today was Friday, and it was the last class before school let out for the weekend, plus it was a game day. It was understandable that they were getting excited.

That didn't make my paranoia or nerves, react any better.

I shuffled into the classroom and came to a sudden halt when I found nearly the entire room full to bursting.

The bell hadn't even rung yet, and it was this full?

Why?

Every single desk in the room was filled, and two older boys were standing.

"Wow," I murmured as I took everyone in. "I'm impressed that everyone is here and seated already."

"That's because if we're late, Coach McDuff kicks our a…"

I gave Johnson a level look. "Don't."

He pretended to zip his lips and throw away the key, causing me to roll my eyes.

The kid was a sweetheart, and cute as a button. I remembered when he was still a boy and he had that head full of curls.

I used to babysit him in the church nursery, and Johnson McDuff Berey had immediately curled himself in my lap the moment he'd entered the nursery doors.

From there, I'd play with those baby soft curls and dream of one day having a little boy exactly like him.

And now he was so grown and taller than me to boot.

"I was under the impression that this was a senior class," I said softly to Johnson.

Johnson grinned. "It helps to have the coach be your uncle. He was able to work me into his class…before they decided to utilize his services elsewhere."

I frowned. "Utilize his services elsewhere?"

He nodded. "Didn't they tell you that he's taking over helping the new track coach? That's why he's not teaching this class. Apparently, Coach Casper isn't able to keep up with all the demands of the track team."

It kind of annoyed me that they'd lied to me about why Ezra wasn't able to teach this class, but again, I was one of the newest hired along with the new track coach. A track coach who, might I add, wasn't in the least bit unable to do her job. Likely, she was just pulling the overwhelmed card to get Ezra to help her.

I swallowed and looked away, searching for something, anything, to get my mind off of those two.

I hated Coach Casper. She was a douche canoe and hated me.

I'd never done anything to her, but you trip a chick one time, causing her to drop her coffee on her new shoes, and she hates you.

Coach Casper hadn't even given me the chance to apologize.

Using the time to collect myself, I pulled the chair out from under the desk at the front of the room and rolled it in Johnson's direction. "Sit here until we can find you a new desk. You there, take that tall chair in the back of the room."

The other kid, a boy that'd been standing there talking to Johnson when I'd walked in, gave me a tight smile and headed in the direction I'd indicated.

Once they were all seated, I pointed at the first desk farthest away from Johnson and said, "Introduce yourself."

They did so, one by one, until there was only one.

"I know you, but go ahead so they don't think I'm playing favorites this early in the semester," I ordered Johnson.

Johnson smiled, looking so much like Ezra that it made my heart hurt.

"Johnson McDuff Berey. I'm the star of the Devil Dogs, and I play first base. I have a hot a—"

"Johnson, you finish that sentence, and I'll take your ass to the field house," a dark, deep, menacing voice said from directly behind me.

I squeaked and jumped, whirling around as I did, putting as much space in between Ezra and I that I could with the distance that the desk behind me afforded.

He looked at me like I'd hurt his feelings.

I kind of felt bad, but I couldn't help my reactions.

They were what they were, and there wasn't a damn thing that I could do about it. I would know—I'd tried.

"You scared the dickens out of me," I whispered.

He studied me like I was a bug.

I knew he was trying to place how he knew me.

Luckily, I'd done a damn fine job at covering my nearly blackened eyes.

It'd been two whole weeks that they'd had to heal, and goddamn if they were taking their sweet ass time.

It was pretty darn sad that his nephew knew me, but he didn't.

I mean, the man had practically seen me do the splits in front of him. Then he'd dropped a box of condoms on me making me bleed...how could you forget that?

Then again, I'd taught Johnson just last year.

I knew that Ezra still couldn't place me, and I had a feeling it was likely due to my school attire, and the fact that my hair was down concealing my face.

Then again, it could be that he didn't recognize me without all the blood...

"I brought you my notes," he said. "Ms. Crusie, yes?"

I nodded, taking the notes he handed me with shaking fingers.

When he didn't immediately let them go when I tried to take them, I dropped my hand.

He frowned.

What, was he expecting me to play tug o' war with it?

He shook the papers impatiently this time, and I resisted the urge to take them on general principle at this point. "You can set them down on the desk."

He narrowed his eyes.

I skirted around the desk and walked to the door, waiting there patiently for him to leave.

Once he was gone, I'd lock the door—just like school policy dictated.

Until then, I waited while he stared me down like I was in trouble.

"Is there anything I can help with?"

I shook my head. "No."

He blew out a breath. "In that case, I'm going to go."

Good for you.

Instead of saying my inner thoughts aloud, I only smiled serenely.

Or tried to.

I think it came out more as a grimace.

When he hesitated next to me in the doorway, I had to fight the urge to squirm.

He was giving me his coach stare, the one I'd seen him pull out for wayward students that miss-stepped in his presence.

I licked my suddenly dry lips and looked at him.

I saw the moment that recognition lit his eyes, but then a woman called his name.

The slut bag, Coach Casper.

"Hey, McDuff. You ready?" Coach Casper called out, sashaying down the hallway. "I got you a coffee and a cookie from the coffee shop in town. Your favorite! Black with one sugar, and an oatmeal raisin cookie."

Ezra hesitated, his eyes still locked on mine, but then the bell rang.

"Coach McDuff?"

He made the decision then and stepped out of the doorway.

I took the opportunity for what it was and went to lock the door with my ring of keys, only I dropped them. When I bent down to pick them up, I slapped my forehead onto the door handle.

Ezra stopped, turning back around, but I hastily picked the keys up, closed the door, and then locked it before he could make it back to me.

I looked at him through the small window pane of glass and saw that he was worried and amused.

I looked away and found the class staring at me.

"Your head's gonna have another bruise tomorrow," Johnson pointed out.

I shrugged it off. "If all I get is a bruise on my forehead today, I'll count myself lucky."

Normally it was worse.

The class laughed.

Then they continued to laugh as I bumbled my way through the first lesson.

Apparently, I wasn't doing them any good—which they shared with me.

All of them knew everything that I'd taught them.

Shit.

It was sad when sixteen and seventeen-year-olds were more experienced than their sex-ed teacher.

CHAPTER 4

Guess what? Chicken butt.

-Text from Raleigh to Camryn

Raleigh

I smiled at the parent, waiting patiently with my hand on the door as the little boy—Alfred—muddled his way to the front seat coming up from the very back. Then, just when he'd gotten to me and I reached out to lift him from his mother's van, he turned around and said, "My backpack!"

I glanced at the mother who was on her phone and clearly didn't want to be bothered.

Some parents really had this drop-off line shit down. Their kids were dressed—with shoes on—and waiting patiently with their backpacks on their shoulders to be let out of the car.

And then there were people like Alfred and his mother. Alfred had to put on his shoes. Then he had to put his papers in his bag. Then he had to find the pencil that had rolled out of his seat and onto the floor somewhere. Then, finally, he'd come up to the front only to have to turn around and go back to the back for the backpack that he'd left behind.

I had to question why I was even over here in the first place.

I taught at the high school. But, once a week, I was forced to come over here since I was what was considered the 'float teacher.' After my morning classes, I was floated around to all the campuses.

Since the high school and the elementary campus were so close together, they didn't see a problem with me having to come all the way over.

No other teacher had to do it.

Just me.

"Go, Tit!"

I blinked, then shook my head, thinking I was hearing things.

"All right, Tit!"

Tit?

Who was he calling Tit?

Alfred jumped down out of his mother's van and landed straight on my foot.

I closed my eyes and tried not to cry out in pain, taking a step forward just as the boy's mother practically peeled out of the parking lot in her haste to leave.

"Sorry, Tit," Alfred apologized. "I didn't mean to."

I didn't bother to ask him to clarify the 'Tit' name. There was no time.

I smiled through clenched teeth. "It's okay."

It wasn't okay.

But I'd get over it.

After walking Alfred up to the front walkway, I went back to my car lane and realized that Alfred was the last of the morning drop-offs.

How had I missed that?

I looked down at my watch.

I had exactly twelve minutes to go get my car and drive over to the high school to be on time for my first class.

I took a step in my car's direction just as another voice had me stopping—this one a lot more welcoming than Alfred's.

Not that Alfred bothered me—he just wasn't *this* particular little girl.

"Hi, Ms. Crusie!" the little girl hollered.

I turned, a smile already on my face, and blinked rapidly.

Why?

Because little Moira Berey, Ezra's niece, was standing there with none other than her Uncle Ezra right beside her.

"Hi, Moira!" I said, smiling a little bit shyly. "How are you today?"

My gaze went from Moira to her uncle, and I had to clench my belly in reaction to his beautiful eyes aimed my way.

Ezra McDuff's eyes seemed to bore right through me, and I looked away.

It'd been a few weeks since our first encounter in his sex-ed classroom, and I had to say that I hadn't faired any better in the weeks following that. The class never got easier, mostly because the topics got harder.

"Ms. Crusie, did you see my hooker boots?"

I blinked. "Your…what?"

"My hooker boots!" She turned and showed me her high-heeled boots, that were actually quite adorable on her, and preened.

I glanced from the 'hooker boots' to the uncle, and back again.

Ezra was too busy looking up at the sky to notice that I was staring.

"Moira, swear to God. I told you not to tell anybody that!"

My lips twitched.

"Why not? I love my hooker boots!" she paused. "But probably not as much as my shit-kickers. I can't decide. I think I like my shit-kickers better because I can get dirty in them. Uncle Ezra said I can't wear these when we're at the park because I might step in goose shit."

I covered my mouth when Ezra started to curse to the heavens.

"Um, darlin'?" I paused. "We probably shouldn't say 's-h-i-t' at school."

"What does s-h-i-t spell?"

I bit my lip to keep the laughter from bubbling out.

"Shit."

I wasn't sure if she was cursing just to curse or cussing to explain the word I'd spelled. Either way, I couldn't contain the smile.

"Alrighty, then," I said as I smiled down at Moira. "I have to go to school, girl. Good luck on your spelling test today."

"You have a spelling test today?" Ezra asked, sounding somewhat alarmed.

Thinking now was a good time to go, I hoofed it as fast as I possibly could across the parking lot and slid into my car without further ado.

After pressing the button on the dash that started my new vehicle up, a *tap-tap-tap-brrrrrr* sounded from it.

I frowned and tried again.

This time the screen on the dash said, "Key Fob Not Detected."

"What do you mean the key fob isn't detected?" I cried, holding the keys up in my hand and dangling them in front of the dash like the car might be able to see that it was, indeed, there.

Pressing the button again, I got another message—this one saying 'Key Fob Battery Low.'

What the absolute fuck?

After one final try, I realized that it probably wasn't going to happen.

What was the freakin' point in getting a new car if the damn thing did exactly what my old one did? At least with my old one, a chartreuse bucket of rust Chevy Silverado, I knew that the damn thing would start—even if it did pour out black smoke the entire time you drove it.

Sure, it was embarrassing, but it got me where I needed to go.

I muttered under my breath as I reached into the back seat for my running shoes.

At least I had those.

This trek across the football field to get to the high school would've been bad if I had to do it in my sandals.

This early in the day, the grass was wet from it being watered every morning around five—I knew the exact time because I was there every single time the water turned on unless it was raining.

I had to get my exercise in somehow.

Toeing off my sandals, I slipped my tennis shoes on sans socks, and said a silent prayer that my shoes wouldn't be too wet for tomorrow due to what I was about to put them through, and got out.

I took off, moving much faster than I probably should have been.

I mean, hello! *Walking disaster, right here!*

After hurrying down the driveway that led to the elementary school, I took a left and headed a little farther up the highway before cutting through the football field.

I'd made it about halfway across the field when my toe caught on a sprinkler head and nearly took me down.

After regaining my balance, I shot forward again, only this time to actually go down hard on the track.

At least it wasn't still wet like the grass, I thought annoyingly.

With only a dark smudge on my gray skirt to show for my recent fall, I decided that maybe it would be better to just be late than it would be for me to hurry any faster. I mean, I could fall, break my jaw, and have to go to the emergency room.

Then I'd be really late!

I'd just pushed through the gate that surrounded the track when Ezra's beautiful Chevrolet parked parallel to the fence.

It—the truck—fit him perfectly.

It was black as midnight and lifted. The only trace of color on the entire truck was the little Chevrolet symbol on the grill, and that was red, white, and blue.

The windows were tinted so dark that I couldn't see him at first.

And, since I could ignore him if I couldn't see him, I hurried past his truck and started walking past it to get into the side entrance of the school when the door opened.

At the perfect time.

I was hit square in the forehead and went down so hard that I didn't even have time to brace for my fall.

One second, I was standing on my feet, and the next I was lying in the dirt staring up at the sky.

"Fuck!" Ezra growled as he hopped out, being careful not to jump out on top of me. "Are you all right?"

Was I all right?

Well, I couldn't feel my face.

I also knew that my nose was bleeding—or would be the moment I stood up.

Right now I could just feel the blood running down the back of my throat.

"Fuck, you're gonna have a bruise," he murmured.

Another one.

My black eyes had healed, and the bruise on my forehead from it meeting the doorknob had finally faded enough to be covered by makeup. But I got a new one every day, so at this point, a bruise was just a bruise. My newest one was on my arm from running into the water fountain of all things. Right now, it was a putrid green that looked like a baby had vomited peas all over my forearm.

I would now be sporting another bruise on my forehead.

Yay.

At least I was getting better with the makeup!

"I'm fine," I lied, pinching my nose as I made my way to stand.

"Are you sure?" he asked, his large palm going underneath my elbow to help steady me.

He needn't have bothered.

I was well versed in the art of picking myself up off the ground.

What I was not well versed in was someone being around for the times that my clumsiness got the best of me.

"I'm..."

He took my hand from my nose, and I immediately felt the blood start pouring out.

He hadn't even hit me in the nose, and it was bleeding.

The traitor.

"Shit," he rumbled. "Let me get you something from my office."

When he turned and ran, I did, too.

Only, he caught up to me when I was at the side door of the school, hand on the lever that would take me inside.

I'd have made it, too, had the damn thing not been locked.

When I went for my keys, he shouted for me to wait.

I didn't.

But he caught up to me anyway.

Damn, the man was just as fast now as he was in high school!

"Wait up!"

I didn't want to wait up. I wanted to run away and hide in the girl's bathroom like I did when I was in high school.

My embarrassment was major.

"I'm going to be late for class," I told him. "And now I have to go to the bathroom and clean up."

He handed me a towel, and I breathed before putting it on my nose.

He grunted in satisfaction and then started to wipe me off with a baby wipe.

A baby wipe?

"I have them in my office for those times when I don't take a shower and can't go straight home," he answered my non-spoken question. "Are you sure you're okay? I thought I saw you get into a car?"

I didn't bother to enlighten him that my car wouldn't start.

Nor would I question why he was watching me get into my car in the first place.

I finally got my keys out of my pocket and punched the right key into the keyhole, turning it at the same time as he continued to wipe down my face.

"Thank you," I said once I got the door open. "You're sweet, but I really have to go."

He grunted something and allowed me to take the baby wipe without too much of a problem.

I felt him following behind me, though.

"What class do you teach next?" he asked.

I tried not to be hurt that he didn't know.

The shithead.

He'd only passed it every single day of his life—and smiled at me at that. *Was the man that unobservant when it came to me?*

I tried not to show him just how dejected I was that he didn't know me even a little bit.

"I'm in the room right next to the office. I'm teaching pre-cal this period," I answered quietly.

"Do you want me to go let them in while you get cleaned up?" he asked.

I shrugged. "I won't be a minute," I said, trying not to sound like I wanted to spend any time with him when I'd like to spend as much with him as possible.

Hell, I'd take getting hit in the face again by his door if it meant that I'd get to spend another ten minutes with him. I was *that* obsessed with the man.

Then, as if she could sense that I was close to spending five minutes with the man, Coach Casper came up and put her hand on Ezra's shoulder. "Heya, Coach!"

I didn't wait around.

I hightailed it to the bathroom and tried not to cry.

What would it take for someone to notice me?

By the time I'd cleaned up in the staff bathroom, I headed hurriedly to my classroom, apologizing profusely once I arrived.

"Sorry, y'all," I apologized to the students that were lining the wall outside my classroom. "Carpool was a pain in the bottom today."

The students didn't care. They were genuinely happy that they had five fewer minutes of class.

"Turn to page sixty-four in your textbook," I said tiredly. "And did you study the chapter like I asked?"

"Yes, ma'am," the class droned.

"Why do we have to go over this again? We learned this last semester."

I looked up to find Quentin Jones, the star JV quarterback and resident funny guy, staring at me with a pained expression on his face.

"Well, if you know all of this, why are you in my class?"

"Because we're required to be here to graduate," Quentin popped off.

I snorted and moved to sit on the edge of my desk.

When I did, it caused the slit in my skirt to hike up slightly—which was of course when Ezra passed by with Coach Casper nipping closely at his heels.

I gritted my teeth as I watched them both sneak into the staff room, and turned back to my class, trying my best to ignore Coach Casper's annoying nasally voice.

"Who wants to show me how to work the first equation?" I asked the class as a whole.

Nobody raised their hands, and I snorted.

"I have M&Ms!" I said, patting a glass jar on my desk that was filled to the brim with the sweet delicacies.

"I like M&Ms, Ms. Crusie," came a deep male voice.

I startled and turned, nearly falling to my butt. I only caught myself just in time to look undignified.

"No way, Coach!" Quentin argued. "Those are ours. You go find your own M&Ms!"

Ezra's lips peeled back into a genuine grin.

I looked past him to see Coach Casper glaring at me.

I would've given her a smug look had she not looked entirely too mad at me for some unknown reason.

"Aren't you supposed to have your classroom door shut at all times, per the superintendent's letter, Ms. Crusie?" Coach Casper asked sweetly, sidling up to Ezra's side.

I swallowed the retort that came to my lips and smiled serenely.

Another student answered for me, though.

"We have one more student coming who's in a wheelchair, Coach Casper. He can't get in with the door closed," Jasslyn, the resident goth, droned monotonously. "In fact, he's right there behind you."

Both Coach Casper and Ezra turned to find Morgan patiently waiting for both adults to move the hell out of his way.

Normally Morgan was very abrupt, but he looked off.

I instantly stood up and started walking toward him.

"Ezra, would you mind staying here for a moment?" I asked, for the first time specifically looking the man in the eye and asking him a question.

Ezra blinked, then nodded, looking taken aback that I'd actually addressed him and given him eye contact at the same time.

He stepped around me and into the room. "I'll catch up with you later, Coach Casper."

Coach Casper turned on her heels and headed back to the staff room, leaving me in the hallway as Ezra passed me in the doorway.

He went to lean on the desk where I was just leaning, and I took the time to move farther down the hall and gesture to Morgan as I did.

"Are you okay?" I asked.

Morgan was a very blunt boy. He didn't care about propriety, and that likely had a lot to do with the situation he found himself in at a very young age.

He was seventeen, and in a sophomore class that he had to retake.

At the age of fifteen, Morgan had been in a four-wheeler wreck that had nearly taken his life. When he'd woken up from the coma he'd been put in to help with the swelling, it'd been to find out that not only was Morgan very hurt, but he would likely never be able to walk again. He was currently paralyzed from the waist down.

He'd missed more than a year of school and was just now getting back to his scheduled classes. So not only was he just now returning, but all of his old friends were seniors this year and leaving him behind.

"I'm fine," Morgan lied. "Can we go inside?"

He looked away and fidgeted, clearly agitated.

"What's a soldier's least favorite month?" I blurted.

I wanted a smile out of this kid's mouth more than I wanted to feel Ezra's attention focused entirely on me.

Morgan had suffered through quite a bit, and it was very rare that I saw the poor thing smile.

"Ms. Crusie…"

I grinned, knowing I had him.

"Fine. What month?" he asked, a small smile popping out over his lips.

"Allich."

He snorted, rolling his eyes like every teenager had before him.

"That's so corny," he grunted. "You ready to teach me something new?"

"Well," I said, walking around the kid. "According to Quentin, there's nothing that I'm teaching today that y'all didn't learn last semester."

I rolled Morgan through the door and to the special table that was put into the classroom specifically for him.

Ezra looked up, interest clearly written on his face, as we entered.

He didn't stop talking about this Friday's baseball game against Center, though.

"...game is at six. I think Ms. Crusie should go, don't y'all?" Ezra asked cheerfully.

"Nooooo!" every single one of my students replied, even Morgan.

I froze for a whole two seconds, before shaking my head. "Y'all don't want me there. I'm bad luck."

The entire room broke out in laughter, and they all took turns explaining just how bad of luck I really was.

Seriously, every single game I went to, whether it be football, soccer, baseball, or volleyball, all turned into a loss for our school.

I would not be attending any games in the foreseeable future.

At least, the students didn't want me to, anyway.

I knew that just as well as they did.

"There was this one time that Ms. Crusie walked through the door of the volleyball game," Andrea started. "She entered through the right-side doors and tripped and fell on a rug. When she fell, the drink she'd been holding spilled, causing the mascot to slip and fall, too. The sign he was holding went sailing across the court and knocked our middle blocker out cold. She ended up needing six stitches."

Then it was Quentin's turn.

"Last year, Ms. Crusie went to our junior varsity game against Tidestell. Do you remember Coach Roby telling you about how that 'dumb lady with the heart of gold' knocked out his star player? That was Ms. Crusie's fault. Apparently, she tried to toss him a bottle of water, and it slipped through his hands and nailed him in the throat. He couldn't catch his breath the rest of the game."

Ezra's eyes turned to survey me.

"She caused an accident, eh?"

I felt my face flame.

I caused a lot of accidents.

"All right," I swallowed. "It's time to get to work. Coach, thank you for sitting with my class for a moment."

Ezra got up from where he was leaning against my desk, and the entire thing creaked when his bulk was lifted free.

I swallowed.

Just standing beside it, my desk that seemed so massive to me looked quite tiny and delicate compared to him.

He started walking toward me, and I went to move out of his way at the same time he grabbed my hand and tugged me with him.

I gave my class a look over my shoulder. "Flip to the correct pages and start working the equation in Test 2B."

Groans followed my exit, and I was smiling when I finally came to a halt right outside the door.

That was when I realized that Ezra McDuff was still holding my hand.

His fingers wrapped clear around my wrist and overlapped themselves. Our skin couldn't be more different. I had pale, pasty white skin where he had rough, tanned skin. He looked like he was outside all day everyday—which he was. I looked just like I stayed inside and didn't dare venture out—which I didn't.

Venturing out meant accidents and running into people that called me the plague.

That just wasn't for me.

That, and I really loved to read. It was hard to read when there was direct sunlight glaring across your screen.

"Is Morgan all right?" he asked.

I melted a little bit at the concern in his voice.

"Yes," I replied, smiling. "He's okay. Well, he could be better, but I think he's going to make it."

He blinked. "I haven't seen him in months. Not since his accident...he looks bad, Raleigh."

I blinked.

That was the first time I'd ever heard him use my name. I hadn't even realized that he *knew* my name.

He'd only ever called me Ms. Crusie.

"I know. But each day he gets a little bit better. I'm keeping an eye on him, and hopefully he'll trust me if he ever has any problems," I murmured.

I knew, better than anyone ever knew, what it was like to be an outsider in this very school.

It was hard to be in the shadows, looking in while everyone else moved to a different beat all around you.

I couldn't tell you how many times that I'd wished it was me sitting beside Ezra and not the captain of the cheerleaders, Sonny Sharlin. I'd watched them go to prom and homecoming. I'd watched him give her a massive mum and her wear it with pride. I'd been that weird girl that sat outside to eat her lunch—if she even ate at all.

So yes, I knew that Morgan felt like an outsider. I saw the girl that sat on the stairs during lunch instead of joining the kids at the picnic tables in the courtyard.

I *was* them not so long ago.

"If you need anything, or think he needs to talk to a man...you can let me know. I'm more than willing to help."

I smiled a little bit sadly. "I'll be sure to let you know if he ever requests it."

Which he wouldn't.

I'd be lucky if Morgan ever said a word to me about anything that was concerning him.

After today, I knew that I was going to have to watch him a little bit better, too.

I didn't trust that look in his eyes.

Not even a little bit.

"Okay." He smiled and finally let go of my wrist.

I looked down at my hand and wondered if the feeling of heat and comfort surrounding that small part of my body would ever feel the same again. I was betting not.

I was touched, willingly, by Ezra McDuff.

I would've snickered had that not been my fantasy.

The poor guy had no clue that he'd just given me the world.

He was paying attention to me, and I wasn't embarrassing myself—being the reason he was paying attention.

Win-win.

His eyes changed. "Do you want to…"

"Hey, Coach!" Coach Casper called from the break room. "Do you want some coffee to go?"

When Ezra turned, so did I.

Who was I kidding? I'd never be anything more than a last resort.

Lani Lynn Vale

CHAPTER 5

I'm into fitness. Fitness taco into my mouth.

-T-shirt

Ezra

"You do know, right, that the teacher that took over your sex-ed class is absolutely terrified to be in there with us, right?"

I looked over at my nephew. "No. What are you talking about?"

"Just come watch her today. You'll see. She's like a tiny mouse in a room full of tomcats."

I frowned as I poured my coffee, wondering what exactly he was speaking about.

She'd been covering my sex-ed class for a while now. Months. And she still hadn't gotten used to it?

"Okay," I paused. "Are you planning on taking your gear or do you want me to bring it with me like I did last time?"

Grady came into the kitchen before Johnson could answer and glared at me. "I made that coffee for me, fucker."

I shrugged my shoulders. "It's my coffee pot."

Grady grunted and then pulled the coffee pod out of the Keurig and tossed it into the trash at the end of the counter. Moments later, he took another fresh pod out of the stand underneath the coffee pot and inserted it before turning to me.

"If you don't want to bring his gear, I will," he said, rubbing his eyes. "I have to come pick up Moira from school around three, and then I can drop it off." He leveled his son with a look. "If he's got it ready to go that is."

Johnson set his bowl down into the sink. "Of course, I have it ready to go, Dad."

Then he calmly walked out of the room.

I snorted.

"Ten bucks says he hasn't even pulled it out of the washer yet," I commented.

"Ten bucks says it's still just as dirty right now as the day he took it off and threw it on the floor in his room after his game," Grady countered.

I snorted.

He was going to lose that one. Mostly because when I'd seen my sister pick up his room, I'd given her my laundry to do, too.

"I saw his mother picking up his floor for him," I explained.

"What's this hullabaloo about a teacher being a chicken and your sex-ed class?" he asked, sighing when his cup of coffee finally finished brewing.

I took a sip of my own coffee. "I asked for my sex-ed class to be taken over due to them tossing more responsibilities when it came to field maintenance on my shoulders. They found another teacher to take over the class. Johnson was saying that she's scared to teach it."

Just saying it sounded as ridiculous as it was.

Who would be scared to teach a sex-ed class? It was basic. Something that every single person in the world should know, even young, stupid kids in high school.

"Who is this teacher?" he asked.

I found myself smiling. "Her name is Raleigh..."

"Crusie," Grady finished for me. "Holy shit. I haven't heard about her in a long time. Since when does she work at the school?"

I frowned. "I don't know...why do *you* know her?"

Grady took a sip of his coffee and grimaced at the heat. "She graduated a year or two behind us. We shared the same homeroom class our senior year...remember?"

No.

No, I did not.

"Are you sure?" I questioned.

He nodded. "Sure as fuck. She was also in another class with us, but for the life of me I can't remember which one. All I know is that you kicked her out of her seat, and the poor girl was blind as a bat and always used to ask me what was written on the screen."

I didn't remember.

But Grady had a mind like a steel trap. If he said it happened, then it did.

"What'd she look like?" I asked.

"Small, gangly, no boobs. Plain hair. Big glasses." He paused. "She got her eyes fixed halfway through that year. I remember asking her why she didn't wear them anymore. You remember them pulling a Carrie on her during prom, right?"

I frowned, trying to think back to prom. I'd been drunk as fuck that day, and I couldn't remember half of what had happened. Prom hadn't been my favorite past time, but only because my high school girlfriend had told me she was pregnant, and she wasn't sure who the father was. "What?"

That'd been a bad day, but luckily a few days afterward, my prom date had informed me that she got her period and that we could continue on as we'd been doing before prom. I'd immediately told her to go screw the man she'd cheated on me with, Cody James.

Speaking of the devil…

"Cody James asked her to prom, and she went. Was dressed in that long Cinderella dress that Sonny spilled punch on, remember?" he pushed.

Now *that*, I remembered.

I didn't remember the girl, so to speak, but I did remember the incident.

My date, Sonny, had tripped. She'd fallen into the punch bowl and the bowl had tipped over, spilling its contents on a lower classman that had come with my rival, Cody James. I hadn't paid her a second thought.

But now I felt bad.

I remembered the way that dress looked. I also remembered her hurrying out of the gym and not coming back. Cody James had started flirting with Sonny's best friend, Eliza. Then Eliza and Cody had fucked in the janitor's closet.

"Ouch," I acknowledged. "That sucks. I do remember that."

Mostly.

"Yeah, heard she rented that prom dress and had to pay eight hundred bucks for it because the lace was stained red. Do you remember that time that that girl got ran over in the school parking lot?" Grady continued.

"Yes," I confirmed, a knot of worry filling my belly.

"That was her—the one that was run over—not the one that was doing the running over. She was walking to her car and the school principal backed up and ran her over. Broke her hand and some kind of internal injuries," Grady reminded me.

I remembered that well. Principal French had gotten fired over that one.

The girl had spent a month in the hospital and had returned looking like a scalded cat who looked like she'd gone ten rounds with Mike Tyson.

"Holy shit," I said. "How did I not know this?"

Poor Raleigh. I felt awful. The poor thing sure the fuck didn't have a great high school career, that was for sure—at least not that particular year anyway.

"Because you were stuck up Sonny's ass—literally and figuratively—and didn't pay attention to anyone or anything but her and football in high school."

My sister came breezing into the room. "You were a pretty awful person."

I snorted. "You liar."

I wasn't an awful person. I'd just been preoccupied at the time, trying to get a scholarship and take care of my family while also trying to make good grades, and have a social life.

It definitely hadn't been easy.

"I'm not a liar. Grady, am I a liar?"

Grady held up his hands in surrender. "Baby, that's my best friend. You're my wife. I am so not getting into the middle of this. And anyway, I'm tired as fuck."

Grady did look tired.

He also was asked repeatedly to find a different job, but the money was good for this one, and it was kind of hard for a father of four to take a lower paying job when the one he had gave him two weeks off and gave him an extra two grand a month to blow how he saw fit.

"Mom!" Johnson called, interrupting our discussion. "I can't find one of my red socks in the washer. Did you happen to wash it and put it away already?"

I held out my hand to Grady, and he slapped ten bucks into it, looking annoyed with his kid.

"The last time I saw it, it was on the floor in your room. I put it on your desk so you wouldn't forget about it."

Grady looked at me expectantly.

"I'll give you two back," I countered.

He shook his head. "I think it should be half. We were both right."

Truthfully, we were. And his son obviously had the same instincts.

"I gotta get going," I said as I walked to the front door. "Am I taking Moira today, or are you, Grady Goulash?"

He flipped me off. "That was old in the sixth grade. Why do you insist on continuing to call me by that ridiculous name?"

I grinned.

"Momma called you Grady God last night," Moira came breezing into the room. "I heard her screaming it."

Everyone in the room took a few moments to digest those words.

"That's fucking disgusting." Johnson gagged as he came shoving shit into his Gun Barrel issued school duffel bag. "I don't even know what to say to that. I think my brain is broken. How the hell am I supposed to play while you're talking about doing my mother?"

"She was also talking about Daddy's wood," Moira continued as if she hadn't done enough damage. "That she felt that he was as hard as a Louisville Slugger."

I bailed. "You can take your own kid to school. Tell her to forget the rest of it while I'm gone, for the love of all that's holy."

Grady laughed at my back the entire way out the door.

The slimeball.

After using the trip to school to forget what I'd heard by cranking up the classic rock station on Pandora, I arrived at school and made arrangements with the lawn maintenance man to weed eat around the outfield fence. Went through the rest of my day half-assed, and genuinely worried about what I would find when the end of the day came. I wanted to see if what Johnson had said was true.

Despite my hopes that what he'd said wasn't correct, Johnson's words were proven accurate.

Raleigh did look absolutely terrified.

At first, I'd thought that maybe Raleigh was just scared to teach the class.

And, honestly? Maybe she was.

But that wasn't the root of her fear.

She stayed up at the front of the class and asked questions, always being careful to keep the desk in between her and the classroom.

At first, I couldn't tell that there was anything wrong, really. At least not until a football player, Darnell, called Raleigh's name.

"Ms. Crusie?" Darnell called loudly.

Darnell was a big kid. At six feet four inches and two hundred pounds, he was easily the biggest linebacker that we had. He was also about nine inches taller than Raleigh and had a hundred pounds on her.

But, he didn't use his size to intimidate anyone. In fact, he was one of the sweetest kids I knew, despite him having a knack for tackling other football players.

When Raleigh jumped like she'd been slapped, my eyes narrowed.

"Y-yes, Darnell?" Raleigh asked, her voice quivering.

But it wasn't her words that had me worried, it was the way she clenched her hands behind her back.

I could see blood running down her hand and dripping to the floor from where she'd clenched her hand so tightly that her fingernails had breached the skin.

"Do you mind if I use the bathroom?" Darnell asked. "I think something I ate for lunch isn't agreeing with me."

Raleigh waved to him. "Of course. Take the hall pass."

Darnell was up and out of the room faster than I'd ever seen him move.

I had to jump back to keep the door from hitting me. Thankfully, the door being left open meant I could hear what was being said in the room better—this time by the students.

"Did you see how far she jumped when he said her name?" a girl asked.

"Yeah," another girl replied. "I thought this morning she was going to freak when Tracy touched her accidentally."

Tracy was another football player. His real name was Trace Yancy, Tracy for short. He was also a baseball player and *not* the biggest guy on the team.

However, what he lacked in size he made up for in character. The kid was a personality, that was for sure.

"Hey, Coach McDuff!"

I winced at Coach Casper's shouted words.

What was the woman's malfunction? Couldn't she just leave me the hell alone while I was spying?

I knew that the loud voice didn't go unnoticed, either, because not only was Raleigh watching me but so was the entire class.

They were all staring at me expectantly.

Then Raleigh turned around, looking pissed.

But I didn't miss the glare she'd sent in Coach Casper's direction before she turned.

Instead of turning to converse with Coach Casper, I waved at her apologetically and walked in through the open classroom door, closing it snugly behind me to ensure that the other woman didn't get any bright ideas that I wanted to talk.

Once it was closed, I walked up to the corner of my old desk, grabbed a few tissues out of the Kleenex box, and gently placed them in Raleigh's bleeding hand.

She looked at me sharply but didn't let the tissues go.

"Can I help you?" she questioned, looking at me primly.

Or, more accurately, my cheek.

I grinned, happy to see that whatever worries that'd been plaguing her now seemed to have fled.

"I'm here to help you go over the lesson for today," I admitted, looking up to find my nephew, Johnson, staring at me in concern.

He hadn't lied.

Something about this class absolutely terrified Raleigh to teach.

And I was going to find out what it was.

But first, I had to actually make myself useful so she didn't get suspicious.

"I'm sorry to interrupt, but this is my favorite lecture to have. You don't mind, do you?" I teased, batting my eyes.

Raleigh's eyes went electric.

"N-no," she stuttered.

I felt something in my stomach flutter.

"Cool," I said as I took my baseball cap that said 'Gun Barrel Coach' off and placed it on the top of her desk. Once there, I turned to the class. "This is where you get to ask me whatever question you want, and I'll answer it to the best of my ability. This chapter we're going to go over today is the one where you should be honest and open with your partner. That includes sharing your sexual history, discussing safe sex practices, making sure that your partner is aware and it's consensual, and also being sure that you're very much aware of what you're doing. To do that, you need to be able to have a discussion with your partner. I want you to write a question that you think a sexual partner should ask before sex. Fold it up and then bring it up to the front and put it in my hat. Go."

Everyone started to tear off strips of paper, and I knew this could get out of hand.

Then again, it always did.

The senior class were technically adults, but a lot of them were just as immature now as they were when they were freshmen.

"All right, first question," I said, gesturing for Raleigh to pick.

Raleigh pulled out her chair, took a seat, and took a deep breath. Then she pulled out a strip of paper folded so many times that it was hard to see and unfolded it.

Her face flushed a bright red the moment that she read it.

"What is the largest thing a woman can fit inside of her?" Raleigh read, choking slightly on the first few words.

I blinked, then shrugged. "A baby."

A couple of the students at the back started to snicker.

"Next question." I grinned at Raleigh.

Raleigh reached for another.

And again, she choked.

"Is it better to have anal or vaginal sex?" she read, sounding extra squeaky.

I bit my lip to keep from bursting out laughing—not because of the question itself, but what that question did to Raleigh's face.

I turned to the class at large. "I'm going to be completely, one hundred percent honest with you. If you have a willing partner that trusts you, both sexual acts can be very satisfying. It's up to you to decide which one—if either—you like best. Next?"

Raleigh squeaked so cutely that I wanted nothing more than to expound on my answer just to hear what she'd say—or do—next.

Wrong time, wrong place.

A couple of the girls in the class giggled, as a couple of the male students grunted.

I rolled my eyes.

The entire damn class was filled with my football team, with more than half of them being on the baseball team. This was nothing I hadn't already heard, in one form or another, from them before.

I was always quite open with my students—and had been—since I'd started teaching this class and realized the importance of it.

"How many calories are there in semen?"

I had no idea.

That was a new question, even for me.

"Uhhh," I hesitated. "I don't know."

"Hey, Google."

I spun around and faced Raleigh, who had a Google device on her desk. "How many calories are in semen?"

The girl was all around surprising.

Then the damn thing answered her.

In a robotic feminine voice, it said, "Each teaspoon of ejaculate has about five to seven calories."

Everyone, even Raleigh and I, laughed.

"Maybe we should just read these to your Google, Mizz Crusie," came Johnson's response.

I rolled my eyes. "Yes, we could do that, but then it's possible you wouldn't get honest answers. And I want you to have nothing but the truth."

"So help you God?" Raleigh whispered, almost to herself.

I snorted and bumped her with my hip, then moved to her desk and propped half of my ass right next to her.

"Next?"

"If you have sex underwater, will the baby be a mermaid?" Raleigh tried valiantly not to laugh, then answered that one herself. "No, mermaids aren't real. However, sex underwater is still unprotected sex. It can, in fact, result in a baby. It just won't be cool like a mermaid."

I found myself grinning.

"Next?" I asked.

She pulled out two more. "Last two."

I held my hand out for one of them and opened it for her before placing it on the desk beside her elbow.

My fingertips brushed the skin of her arm and she said, "You touched my weenis."

I blinked. "I touched your pen…what?"

"Weenis. Weenis is also known as the skin of your elbow. See?" She pointed at her elbow, then pinched the loose skin there.

"Oh," I paused. "Good to know."

She bit her lip, then looked away quickly, clearing her throat.

But before I could tease her about her 'weenis' or answer the last two questions, the bell rang. "I'll answer these at the beginning of next session so I don't interrupt Ms. Crusie's next class."

"Yes, Coach," the class replied.

After a myriad of 'bye, Ms. Crusie, bye, Coach McDuff,' the class finally emptied of its occupants, leaving me and the silent woman sitting next to me completely alone.

"That was fun," I replied.

She rolled her eyes and stood up, reaching down to collect her papers that were half under my ass.

I didn't move.

Not until she turned her eyes up to me, and even then, it was to grab her wrist so she couldn't go any further away.

"Go to the baseball game with me tonight, then have dinner with me."

She blinked.

Blinked some more.

Then burst out laughing.

CHAPTER 6

My PEN IS bigger than yours.

-a note from student to student in Raleigh's class

Raleigh

"Why me?" I asked bluntly once I'd regained my composure. "I'm nobody. Is this a pity party date or something?"

He wasn't being serious.

Ezra McDuff, heartthrob and star in my own private fantasies for more years than I could count, was not asking me out on a date.

Hell had frozen over.

"Come on," he urged, his eyes genuine. "Please? Is it so hard to believe that I find you pretty, and want to take you out to dinner?"

I didn't want to tell him no.

I'd tell him yes every single time.

Do you want to come to the moon with me, Raleigh? *Yes, I'll fly to the moon with you every day and twice on Sunday if only you asked it.*

Will you loan me eight thousand dollars? *Sure, let me borrow against my 401k. It takes two days. Is that okay?*

I need bone marrow from a child that's of my blood. Will you have my babies?

"Raleigh?" Ezra urged.

I blinked, startled.

"Yes, I'll have your babies," I blurted.

His face split into a wide grin. "That's not quite what I asked."

I felt like I was going to vomit.

That did not just come out of my mouth.

I looked at him wide-eyed. "What did you ask again? I'm afraid I got lost when you told me I was pretty."

His smile turned soft. "I asked if you'd go to the baseball game with me, and then go out for a bite to eat afterward."

So nowhere near 'have my babies.' Got it.

"I don't know..." I hedged. "Me and sporting events aren't really a good idea. The students weren't joking. They all look at me like I have the plague when it's mandatory that I attend. You should've seen the last event that I was forced to help chaperone. Everyone was on their best behavior because they thought I was going to ruin it if they did anything to garner my attention."

He snorted and scooted minutely closer.

"I promise that it's not going to be bad. You don't need to show up until the end of the game," he said. "And you can hide in the back by the dugout. They'll never even see you unless you come around the wall."

I frowned. I could do that...

"All right," I acquiesced. "But if this goes bad, you only have yourself to blame."

He winked at me. "It'll be fine. You'll see."

In two hours, he'd be choking on those words.

***

Ezra

"Johnson," I bellowed. "Pull your head out and play *ball!*"

As a coach, I probably shouldn't tell any of my players to 'pull their head out.'

However, they were playing like utter shit. Like we hadn't gone through practice for two months working on the most basic of drills.

Yet, here they were, missing balls left and right, showing me that they weren't near as ready as I thought they were.

A little league team could play better than them right then.

I should also have some more composure than I did, but I couldn't manage to get my shit together.

My day had gone from great that morning after spending it with Raleigh, to absolute and utter shit the further the day went along.

All of that had to do with the goddamn school board and their refusal to consider building the athletics department a goddamn field house or sporting complex that wasn't falling down to the ground.

Hell, getting new uniforms out of them had been like pulling teeth, and even then, they'd only had to cover the cost of shipping the goddamn things. The damn booster club had raised the money for all the rest.

"Safe!"

I looked at the ump, my blood boiling, and felt my entire body go stiff.

The umpire wasn't helping things. Not only were my boys playing bad, but the umpire was making calls that were clearly in favor of the other team.

"All right, boys. Bring it in!" I called.

My players brought it in, but a whistle from the far side of the dugout had me turning to see the principal there, gesturing me over.

I grimaced when I saw the superintendent of the school district standing beside her.

Son of a bitch.

"All right, boys. Pay attention to the song. Talk quietly amongst yourself. I'll be back." I patted Johnson's hat with the tips of two fingers, and he winked at me.

Normally, I'd have left the team in the assistant coach's hands, but since the assistant coach was busy teaching the JV team currently, they didn't have anyone to distract them while I likely was on my way to getting my ass chewed.

Every step I took in their direction was purposeful and measured.

I'd just about gotten to them when I saw Raleigh at the entrance to the field next to the end of the dugout, trying valiantly to help Morgan Bryce get over the hump that separated the grass from the other side of the fence.

I let out a sigh of relief when I saw what it was the superintendent and the principal had needed.

The weight of Morgan's wheelchair made it nearly impossible to get over the hump.

"You singing for us, Morgan?" I asked, hopeful.

Morgan shrugged. "Yeah."

I laughed. "Don't sound so excited about it now. You might pop a blood vessel in your exuberance."

Morgan snorted. "Help me out here, will ya?"

I went to the back of his wheelchair and finagled him out onto the field, patting his shoulder as I did. "Can you get there the rest of the way?"

I eyed the wheels on the wheelchair, and then the thick grass and dirt that separated him from the microphone that they'd set up for him to sing "God Bless America" and likely "Take Me Out to the Ballgame," too.

"Yeah, Coach. I'll be fine," he said, then started off.

"Thanks," Raleigh said. "I just didn't have the power in my thighs to get him going, and his wheelchair battery is low. Something about the charge not holding? I'm not sure. But you saved the day."

I winked at her, then turned to the other two individuals still standing there.

The superintendent was a big guy, almost as big as me. He could've just as easily helped, but then he might've gotten his shiny loafers dirty or something.

"Mrs. Sherpa. Mr. Powers." I nodded my head at them.

Raleigh hissed in a breath, and I looked at her.

Her eyes were directed at something across the field, and then she was running.

I turned to see what was going on and cursed before starting off after her.

I did have to say, though. Raleigh was quick.

She only tripped over thin air twice before making it to Morgan's side, who was down on his belly in the dirt.

I heard the tail end of the laughter and the not-so-sweet-natured ribbing that a few of the seniors were giving Morgan. More than a few of them were laughing and pointing, not to mention being so loud that even the other team was paying attention.

"Stop it now!" Raleigh growled at my team. "You should be ashamed of yourselves. Instead of laughing that he fell out of his chair, you should be helping him up!"

"Not my fault the dumbass didn't pay attention to what was in front of him," one of the boys muttered.

I arrived at Morgan's other side, and together, Raleigh and I both maneuvered Morgan back into his seat.

"You okay, bud?" I asked him while Raleigh wiped his shirt off.

Morgan wasn't looking at me. He was looking down at his hands.

I could feel him trembling.

He was angry and embarrassed, and it didn't help that the boys continued to tease him as the rest of the high schoolers in the stands behind him laughed at their antics.

"Stop," Raleigh ordered harshly. "All of you *stop*."

Morgan turned so sharply that he was only on two of the four wheels and started motoring back to the entrance of the field— song forgotten.

"That's why we're losing!" I heard a player say from the back. "Ms. Crusie is here. Her and her bad juju, along with Morgan's bad luck are not doing us any favors."

It sounded like Camden, but I wasn't sure without actually turning around and confirming.

Unfortunately, I was too focused on Raleigh's devastated face to take my eyes away from hers. "Wait for me at the dugout, darlin'?"

Raleigh didn't hesitate, looking away quickly. I had a feeling she wouldn't be waiting for me.

The moment she was gone, I caught my sister's eye in the bleachers and gave her a chin lift and nudged my head in Raleigh's direction.

She didn't miss a beat.

That's what I loved about my baby sister. She was always quick to catch on, even though some of those times I didn't want her inside my brain knowing my every thought.

The moment she was gone, I gave a quick look at all the parents.

None of them had said a word, and they were all waiting for me to give a pep talk that I'd been intending to give to their sons.

Well, I wouldn't be doing that. Not after all the bullshit I'd just heard.

I turned to the team.

"I've never been more disappointed in a team of young men more than right now."

A few of the parents, as well as the players, inhaled deeply, surprised that I'd say that. I was a very positive person...*normally.*

Right then, though? I was fucking pissed.

"Coach..." Coach Casper from somewhere behind me said, sounding worried.

I turned my gaze on her and let her know with only a single look to shut it.

She closed her mouth and looked to the principal who was readying herself to interrupt. So I forged forward and let the boys know exactly what I felt about their actions.

"Johnson, do you know the definition of bully?" I asked.

Johnson, my smart nephew, blinked in confusion.

"Uh, a person that picks on someone?" he asked.

I turned to Banks. "What about you? What do you think bully means?"

"When you intimidate a person?" he offered.

I gritted my teeth, then pointed at Johnson. "You are a bully." I turned to Banks. "You are a bully."

I repeated that, over and over again, until I had pointed at every single person that I saw engaging in the torture of the kid.

And it was torture. Their pointing and laughing, although harmless in theory, was devastating to that poor kid. A kid that'd gone through quite enough and shouldn't have to deal with the shit my team had just laid at his feet.

"A bully is not tolerated on my team. Now, every one of you will sit there and watch the junior varsity team play for you. Then, you will go take that uniform off and get out of my stadium. Think about what you did and meet me at the track on Tuesday. I don't want to see or hear from you until then."

"But Coach, there are still three innings..." Rhodes started.

I held my hand up, disgusted. "The junior varsity will play for you."

With that, I walked to the younger boys—who'd won their game played before this one—and gestured the other coach over.

"You mind if I allow my JV team to play? They need the practice and the reward. We'll forfeit the game," I said to the other coach.

He nodded once. "I saw what happened. Brutal but effective."

I shrugged. I didn't want to talk about it to be honest.

I also needed to go get Raleigh, but I had three more innings to get through before that happened.

Allowing my JV to play had been a spur of the moment thought. And honestly, they looked excited as hell to be doing it. The bragging rights alone were going to burn for months.

This game, the senior game, was a big deal. It was the last home game that the seniors would ever play in this stadium. The next time they arrived, it would be as a guest, not a player.

I had a feeling that in about forty-five minutes, I'd be hearing it from the superintendent, the principal, as well as almost all of the senior parents.

Yeah, this was going to be fun…not.

***

Raleigh

I hovered next to the exit, standing next to Morgan who was as stiff as a board in his seat.

He did not look happy to have to wait for his ride, and even more, he could hear a few of the girls snickering about what had just happened behind him.

I wanted to throat punch every single one of them.

Though, with both the principal of the high school and the superintendent of the entire district at the game only a few hundred yards away, I was not going to act on my instincts—which was give the girls a piece of my mind.

Instead, I stayed next to Morgan and tried to think of something to say that would make him understand that it was okay.

"In high school," I said. "The senior class voted me as prom queen. The guy I had a crush on took a girl, my arch nemesis, to the prom. And she went out of her way to spill punch on me and my dress. It wasn't just a glass of punch, it was the whole punch bowl. She then informed me that the only reason my date asked me was so I'd be there to accept my award. The punch was spur of the moment—but that decision cost me eight hundred dollars that I didn't have since I was forced to pay for the dress which was a rental. I was made the laughing stock of the school."

Morgan's startled gaze met mine.

"I used to have the biggest crush in the world on Coach McDuff," I told him, seeing his eyes widen more and more as I spoke. "He laughed at me."

Morgan's mouth fell open.

"He saw me there, red Kool-Aid dripping down my dress, and he laughed." I swallowed, remembering as if it were yesterday. "It broke my heart."

"You should've punched him in the junk," Morgan murmured.

I snorted. "I couldn't even look at him, Morgan. I don't think you understand the intensity of my crush."

And it definitely wasn't past tense. I saw the moment he understood.

"You still like him?" he asked.

I nodded, and felt the first trickle of blood down the back of my throat, announcing an impending nose bleed.

I groaned and started to search through my purse for a tissue.

"Every single day I do something stupid and embarrassing in front of him," I told Morgan. "But you know what?"

I pressed the Kleenex to my nose and hoped that it wouldn't be a bad bleed.

Then again, with it being the middle of spring and the thousands of pollen particles floating through the air, I didn't have high hopes.

"I went to school and did it all over again the next day." I paused. "Ezra's—Coach McDuff's—entire senior year, I sat behind him in one of my classes. He never once noticed me."

Morgan's eyes turned sad.

"I had a crush before this," he gestured at his body. "I haven't had the courage to talk to her since."

I leaned against the chain-link fence and contemplated what I was going to say next. "I know that you think that this is the end of the world…but maybe when you get older, you won't think the same way. Kids…they can be cruel. I know that something Ezra found funny when he was eighteen isn't something he finds funny now. He would not laugh if the same thing happened to me now as he would have back then. The same applies to you…kids will be kids…but eventually, they do grow up and get out of that stage where they're all assholes."

Morgan snorted. "I'm not sure as a teacher you're allowed to call kids assholes."

I shrugged. "If the shoe fits…"

Morgan sighed. "I don't think my ride's going to get here any time soon."

I frowned. "I'd take you home, but I'm fairly sure your wheelchair isn't going to fit into my Honda."

Morgan's lips twitched. "No, I don't think it's going to, either. But my grandma will be here…she will just be late."

"Is that you trying to say that you should go back in and continue to watch the game?" I asked hopefully.

Morgan shrugged. "I guess it won't hurt."

I winked at him, then turned to gesture toward the field. "Let's go."

CHAPTER 7

Yuck Fou.

-Text from Raleigh to Ezra

Raleigh

I was a nervous wreck as I was waiting for Ezra to get to his truck after the game had finally finished.

I'd met his sister on the way back to the game, and she'd offered me a place to sit next to her and her husband.

I'd taken her up on the offer, but only after making sure that Morgan could wheel his wheelchair up next to us.

I was surprised to see that almost every single player that'd been involved in the earlier fiasco had been riding the bench, and even more surprised when Ezra's sister had explained that Ezra had benched every single one of them—senior players included.

And, from what I'd gathered as I'd sat and watched, the players, as well as the parents, had not been happy.

Then again, after the way that the seniors had acted, I didn't see the problem.

The first 'look at that loser' that had come out of their mouth had made me stiffen. The 'leave him down there and let him piss himself in humiliation' had been what had sparked my temper.

Those boys knew better. They knew better, yet they'd hurt Morgan anyway. And I was disappointed in them.

I was biting my lip and contemplating running away when I saw the distinctive shadow of Ezra making his way out of the fieldhouse.

He had a pair of khakis and a navy blue polo shirt on, and his gaze was directed solely on me.

I barely contained the urge to lick my lips.

When Ezra was in high school, he'd been a gorgeous boy, but now? Seeing him as an adult? Holy shit. He didn't have anything special on, and honestly, he wasn't wearing anything much nicer now than he had when he was younger…but he'd definitely filled out in all the best ways.

His biceps were bigger, his jaw was more chiseled, his beard…wow. And those lips of his? I wanted nothing more than to press my lips to his—then again, that had never changed.

"You ready to go grab something to eat?" he asked, sounding tired and worn out.

I tilted my head and studied him. "I'm ready…but you don't look like you are."

His lips twitched up at the corners, but a smile didn't grace his lips like I'd been hoping for.

"I…do you want to go to my place and have some pizza?" he asked hopefully.

Did I? Was I ready for that step?

I knew that he was just being nice, and honestly, what did I have to lose here? This was my teenage fantasy come to life. So what if he was being sweet?

"I could go for pizza," I admitted. "As long as you want me there, that is."

The smile that graced his lips was small this time, but most definitely there.

"You want to follow me?" he asked. "Or I could drive and bring you back to your car later tonight."

"I can drive," I lied. I wanted to ride with him more than I wanted to take my next breath. "You'll just have to drive slow. My night driving skills are a little less awesome than my day ones."

He snorted. "I think you should ride with me, then."

I barely contained my excitement.

"Okay," I breathed.

He walked around to the passenger side of his truck and opened the door, offering me his hand.

I took it and climbed up, very aware of how close he was the entire time.

Once my ass hit the seat, he stared at the hole in my pants, just over my knee, for a few long seconds, before his face turned up and his eyes met mine.

"I had a really bad day," he told me. "And I'm glad that you stayed."

Then he touched one fingertip to the skin that was poking out of the hole and then backed up before closing the door softly.

I swallowed and felt my belly fill with butterflies.

He rounded the hood of the truck and hopped into his seat easily, automatically reaching for his seat belt as he turned to survey me.

"You okay?" he questioned.

I swallowed and nodded. "I did tell you that they think I'm bad luck..."

He snorted. "Somebody tells you that enough, I'm sure at some point you're going to start believing it. A person isn't bad luck...though, just sayin', baseball players do consider their superstitions very important to them."

I snorted. "Oh, I know that."

His brows rose. "You do?"

I nodded. "My brother played."

"Your brother?"

I nodded. "He, uh, died when I was eighteen. He was two years younger than me in school. His name was Gavin."

Ezra's face instantly changed.

He'd heard about Gavin.

Everybody in the town of Gun Barrel had heard about Gavin.

You only had to live here for a week to find out what happened to Gavin.

Why?

Because Gavin was the boy that died in the middle of a baseball game his junior year, and we had a sculpture of him in the middle of the city park, and a plaque at the school, as well as a wing at the hospital dedicated to him.

"That was your brother?"

I nodded.

"I heard about a boy that died, and his parents were the ones to buy us the HeartGuard shirts," Ezra murmured.

I felt my stomach tighten.

That'd been my brother's contribution—my eldest brother, Croft, anyway.

Gavin had been playing mid-season. He'd come up to bat his second time, and the pitcher had thrown a wild pitch and struck him in the chest. The ball had made contact with his heart at *just* the right moment—according to doctors—and his heart had stopped.

He'd died in the middle of that field, and despite the coach at the time, as well as my own father, giving him CPR, he hadn't made it.

Gavin's passing was also why almost every single sports complex in all the schools had defibrillators—just in case something tragic like that happened again.

"Shit," he murmured. "I should've put two and two together."

I smiled and looked down at my lap. "It's hard for that to happen. I was always very shy and introverted while Gavin was the life of the party. We didn't look like each other, and we certainly didn't hang out with each other. It's easy to see how you missed it."

He looked at me with a wry smile on his face. "Gavin Crusie is an unusual name. There is only one set of Crusies in this town, and that's your family. Everyone knows the Crusies...I should've put two and two together. Trust me. I feel stupid."

My lips twitched. "You were a big kahuna star quarterback Superman for the Sooners at the time of his accident. There's no way that you would've known when you were busy winning the..." I trailed off, wondering if I should relay my obsession with him.

"I know," he murmured. "We may have won the college championships, but it's hard not to hear about that happening. My whole family told me. It was a big deal."

It was a big deal.

In fact, it still was a big deal.

Every time baseball season came around again, my family made a big production about making sure that they got each player a HeartGuard shirt in the area, college and high school—at least Croft did, anyway.

Croft was a lawyer and had been one for two years when Gavin had passed. He had money to burn, and he used it to make sure that nobody in Gun Barrel ever had to get the same call that he did that fateful day.

It was surreal, watching your brother—who was at peak health— fall to his knees and then to his face. Then, to attend his funeral just two days later.

I'd literally been talking to him twenty minutes before that game and had asked him if he could help me with my car the next morning. He'd tweaked my nose and given me a kiss on the cheek before running out on the field.

I could still remember the way he'd squeeze my head in between his massive arms when he gave me hugs just like it was yesterday, and not years ago.

"I'm sorry, Raleigh," Ezra whispered into the quiet cab.

I smiled. "He died doing what he loved…we lost him too soon, but who can say that they literally went out doing the one thing that made them happiest in the world?"

Ezra's smile was wistful. "I see where you're coming from, but still."

I patted his hand that was resting on the console between us, then felt like it'd been scalded when he quickly turned his hand over and captured mine.

"Are you still hungry, honey?" he asked.

I nodded. I was.

Talking about Gavin didn't make me as sad as it used to, but that was to be expected.

Now, hearing about my baby brother just made me smile and remember the good times.

There would always be a little bit bad with the good, but you couldn't have flowers without first dealing with the rain.

"How about El Rincon?" he rumbled, not letting my hand go.

I grinned. "El Rincon's is fine…but I think I'd still rather take you up on the pizza if you don't mind."

His eyes warmed as he glanced over at me. "Cool."

That's how, thirty minutes and a pizza later, I found myself curled up on one side of the couch, watching *The Deadliest Catch* with a slice of deliciousness in my hand.

"I'd probably fall right the heck over and never be found again," I murmured, watching as the guys on the boat slipped and slithered while they tried to do their job in the pouring rain and rough seas.

"Even I probably wouldn't be able to hack that," he admitted. "They have a hefty sum they make from that, however. For the money? I might do it—if I didn't have a family to worry about at home."

I looked over at him. "You have a family in here somewhere that you're hiding?"

I'd looked around his place when I'd gotten there, and what I'd found was a whole bunch of nothing.

He had a one-bedroom, one-bath mother-in-law suite with a small kitchenette. Hell, it didn't even have a closet. Just the bare necessities.

All his clothes were in a cube-like storage system—I would know because I'd snooped when he'd gone into the bathroom and taken a quick shower—there was officially nowhere he could hide anybody in this place.

He hooked his thumb up and said, "Cady—my sister. She lives on the other side of this wall with Grady, Moira, Colton, and Johnson."

"Didn't your sister have four?" I asked.

He nodded. "They do—Maden. He's in college now in Alabama."

I shook my head. "I want all my kids to be close together. Three of them. I think an age gap like the one your sister and Grady have with their kids might very well kill me."

He snorted. "I think it killed Cady a little bit inside, too. But, Moira is a cute, perfect kid. Literally, if they had to end on one, Moira was the best way to tie up that chapter in their lives."

I grinned. "Did she have her tubes tied?"

He nodded. "And Grady had his snipped, too. I think they didn't want to chance it."

I wouldn't either.

I shivered. "My brothers had a large age gap between them— almost ten years. Gavin was the youngest at two and a half years younger than me. Croft is the oldest. Seven years after Croft, I came along. I think I want them even closer than that. Maybe a year and a half. Irish twins would be perfect, too."

He frowned. "Irish twins?"

I took a bite of my pizza, then turned a little bit in my seat so I could see him without turning my face. "Irish twins are children born in the same year."

His eyes widened. "So, you get pregnant almost right away after the previous pregnancy. That'd be some hard shit right there.

Moira is tough. I can't imagine having to deal with another that close in age to her."

I didn't know what to say to that, so I just took another bite of pizza and turned my attention back to the television.

My butterflies hadn't abated since I'd arrived, and I still couldn't figure out what to say to him.

I couldn't believe that I'd told him about how many kids I wanted—little did he know that I'd known exactly how many I wanted—with him—since I was a freakin' freshman in high school.

Out of everything that I'd wanted in my life, there was one thing that had stayed constant since I'd been that young, naïve girl—and that was the knowledge that Ezra was my unicorn. The man that I wanted above all others, and I knew nothing else would ever do.

I couldn't tell you why.

I just knew that he'd been that one for me—and probably always would be.

As a result, to be in his place, sitting on his couch, eating pizza only three feet away from him? Yeah, you could say there was an epic meltdown waiting to be had the moment I walked in my door.

I couldn't wait to tell Camryn about this.

Camryn had been privy to my crush since she was right there, crushing right along with me to Ezra's best friend—Grady. It'd been a sad day for both of us when our dream of marrying best friends had died a slow, tragic death. But, it worked out for the best because I could tell that Cady and Grady were made to be together.

Camryn would one day find her unicorn man…and she'd still be excited that I'd actually been in my unicorn's house.

Even if I had made a fool of myself by telling the man that I wanted three children, all of them within two years of each other.

"Last piece, do you want it?"

I looked over to find Ezra holding out a slice of pizza as if it was the holy grail.

I shook my head. "No, thank you. I've already had three. If I eat anymore, I'll pop."

That was also a lie.

I wouldn't pop…what I would do, though, was make a fool of myself.

I was already feeling as if I needed to unbutton my jeans.

Adding in that fourth piece, on top of being nervous as hell, didn't seem like the best of ideas.

Just as I was about to shift into a more comfortable position—because my God, what the hell was I thinking wearing my tightest pair of freakin' jeans?—a big boom of thunder rents the air.

Shortly after that, the entire small room around us flickered, made a weird popping sound, and then went completely black.

I winced.

"Uhhh," I murmured. "That sure didn't sound good."

Ezra snorted. "Grady and I did all the wiring on this addition…let's just say, if you ever see that our house has burned down, that's why."

I bit my lip. "That's not good, Ezra."

Ezra snorted and moved in the darkness, heading for what I assumed was his phone that he'd left laying near the TV.

"I'm joking. We had a certified electrician come out and check it over…after," he amended.

I snickered and set my feet back on the floor, my eyes going around the room to try to locate where he was.

Moments later, I saw a lighter flick to life over by the door that led to the main house, and then he was lighting a candle and heading back toward us.

Another boom of thunder filled the air around us, and lightning lit up the entire room like a creepy horror flick.

"After what?" I questioned, sensing he was beating around the bush about his electrician skills.

"After we already caused a small fire," he lamented. "I'm good with a football…but my building skills—at least when it comes to running electrical—could use some work."

I snickered, and he surprised me by setting the candle down hard on the coffee table.

"You want to play some cards?" he asked. "I'd ask if you wanted to go home, but I have a feeling that the storm" —the thunder once again rocked the entire room— "is going to be here for a while. It wasn't supposed to be here for another couple of hours, otherwise, I would've cut it short…you don't mind staying, do you?"

Did I mind staying at my crush's house?

Hell no.

I'd move in if you wouldn't think I was a complete freak.

"That's f-fine," I murmured, feeling the butterflies start to turn into nausea. "What kind of card game?"

Ezra scooted closer, then pulled some cards out of his pocket.

"Have you ever played Speed?" he asked.

I gave him a look that he could barely make out, but he saw enough to laugh. "You're gonna go down."

I snorted. "I used to play with my brothers. Trust me when I say that I'm gonna totally kick your ass."

He moved so that he was on the opposite side of the coffee table from me, then started to set up the card game. After handing me my cards, he waited for me to put them into order before saying, "Ready?"

And that was how we spent our night.

The thunder rumbled overhead, the wind shook the windows, and Ezra and I laughed our asses off.

It was hours later, after consuming a few beers and playing over ten hands of Speed, that I finally admitted defeat.

"I suck!" I laughed, throwing myself backward onto the couch. "I have no clue how I got to be so bad!"

He chuckled. "Don't feel too bad. I practice a lot with the kids. When Grady's gone, they spend more time over here than in their own house."

I smiled and shifted, my pants super uncomfortable.

I groaned and shifted again.

"What's wrong?" he asked.

Thunder boomed so loud that I jumped. "Shit. That scared the crap out of me."

He stood up and stretched and the shirt that he had on lifted up high over his belt, revealing his sculpted abdomen.

He had a six-pack. Oh, dear. Sweet baby Jesus.

I wanted him so bad.

I squirmed in my seat, this time not from my jeans digging into my belly, but because my vagina had pulsed with need.

God, the man was sexy.

"What's wrong?" he repeated.

Instead of telling him the reason I'd squirmed that time, I went with my original discomfort. "My pants are tight as hell, and they're digging into my flab."

He blinked. "You don't have any flab."

I snickered. "Oh, I have flab. Trust me on this."

His eyes narrowed, and he dropped his arms back down by his sides. "I have a pair of sweats you can borrow… or I can offer you a pair of Cady's. She decided that she was going to stop wearing normal pants after Moira was born, and I haven't seen her in jeans or pants of any kind that weren't stretchy since then."

I found myself smiling. "That's kind of funny…and I can handle the jeans. They're just uncomfortable. I don't see us being here too much…"

The tornado sirens started to go off, and Ezra's eyebrows lifted.

I swallowed. "Should we go hide in your bathtub?"

He walked to the cube storage and opened a drawer, pulling out a pair of sweats and tossing them in my direction. "Let me go make sure that my sister heard that, and then I'll be back…and yes, head to the bathroom."

I kept hearing the weatherman in my head saying 'Get to a small, windowless interior room.'

After Ezra disappeared, I started to unbutton my pants, shoving them down my legs moments later.

I'd just stepped one foot into the sweatpants hole when Ezra came back in.

"They're not here. I for…" He halted suddenly halfway in the doorway. "Shit, I'm sorry."

I squeaked in surprise, then fell over onto the couch while I kicked my legs into the pant legs.

Before I could get them both in, I fell to the ground between the coffee table and the couch, hitting hard.

Once I had them pulled up over my hips, I laid there for a few long seconds wishing that the ground would swallow me whole.

"You okay?"

I looked up to find him standing over me.

"I'm just gonna lay here and hope that the tornado only takes out this couple feet of area right here," I gestured to where I was laying.

He snorted and offered me his hand. "If it makes you feel better, I only saw your ass."

No, that didn't make me feel better. Not in the least.

"Swear to God," I told him honestly, hands still covering my eyes. "If you say another word, I might break down in embarrassed tears."

He snorted and I heard him move, then suddenly I was up and moving.

I made an 'umph' sound when my belly hit his shoulder, and shortly after that, I gasped because Ezra was really tall, and I found myself staring down his back and at his ass.

His ass that was encased in a pair of jeans that molded delectably to his ass so perfectly that I wanted to write the makers of Levi Jeans a letter and tell them that they should get an award.

The way his shirt was riding up, I could see a small sliver of skin, and the dark gray outline of his underwear…and then it all went dark because he made it into the bathroom.

"Shit," he said, handing me the flashlight that I only just now realized that he had. "Hold on. I'm gonna go back for the candle. I don't want to run down the batteries on this flashlight."

He turned around, and I found myself going back out into the living room. Moments later he had the candle in his hand as he squatted down, and I got to see the crack of his ass.

And what a nice crack it was!

Jesus, I was such a loser! It was bad when the crack of Ezra's ass turned me on...

A sharp crack of thunder had me gasping, and I grasped what was closest to me...Ezra's butt.

"Shit!" I cried out, my heart pounding away in my chest.

Then I realized what I'd done, and immediately let him go.

"I'm sorry," I murmured. "I didn't mean to touch your butt."

Ezra laughed, and all of a sudden, we were once again in the bathroom, the light of the candle illuminating the entire tiny space.

Ezra set me down on my feet, and then grabbed both towels off the towel rack and started wiping down the small tub that looked to be half the size of a normal shower.

"This is quite a shower," I teased as I turned off the flashlight and set it down next to the candle.

He looked at me over his shoulder and winked, and I tried not to melt into a puddle of goo right there on the floor by his feet.

There was only so much sexy Ezra that I could take...

"I guess that's good enough," he murmured. "Let me go grab the blankets and pillows from the couch. From the sounds of it, we're going to be here a while."

I cleared my throat and said, "Do you mind if I, uh, use the facilities while you're gone?"

He snorted. "Hurry. I don't want to get picked up by the tornado."

I did hurry, because the thought of no longer having Ezra's pretty face to look at actually had my heart panging in my chest.

I may not ever have Ezra, but at least a girl could look.

After washing my hands and yanking the door open, I was surprised to see Ezra standing there with an armful of blankets and pillows. "Where did you get all this?" I asked. "I only saw the one comforter."

He grunted. "I raided my sister's hall closet."

Grinning, I backed out of the way and allowed him to throw every last bit of his burden into the floor of the shower. "Come on," he urged.

I followed him down into the makeshift pallet, and then laughed when I saw him pull out his comforter and bring it over the top of us.

After some situating, he ended up with his back against one side of the tub, and me with mine against the other. His legs were tangled up with mine, and he was chuckling as he tried to find a more comfortable position.

"How does someone as tall as you get into this tub?" I wondered aloud as I scrunched up my feet.

Finally, I just gave up and stretched my legs out over his chest, which he gladly allowed me to do because it gave him way more leg room—legs in which he stretched out on either side of me, one foot going up under one armpit, and hanging out on the other side.

"I am much shorter than you and I barely fit in here." I grinned teasing him. "I take it you don't take baths very often."

He snorted. "I don't have time to take baths. I'm lucky enough to find time to take a shower." He paused. "Sometimes I have to take them at the school."

I could imagine.

"I know you're busy." I giggled. "That's why I had to take over your sex-ed class, remember?"

He scooted himself over a little more, and then he leaned his head back and watched me.

"My nephew told me you were scared to death to teach that class," he said hesitantly. "Are you?"

The blunt honesty in his question had my belly dropping.

I hadn't realized that I'd been that transparent.

"I..." The loud boom of thunder overhead, followed by what sounded like a tree falling, had both of us tensing.

"Shit," I whispered. "Does your sister have any trees?"

Ezra shrugged. "No. Not any that would make *that* sound when it fell."

Both of us waited to see if we could hear more, and while we were waiting, Ezra absently took one of my feet—which were bare—into his hands and began massaging it.

I couldn't help it.

I moaned.

I'd worn my prettiest, sexiest pair of shoes that I could find. However, the downside of the cuteness of those shoes was how freakin' uncomfortable they were.

My toes curled when he hit one particularly sore spot.

"Sore?" he questioned.

I peeked open one eye and nodded at him. "Those shoes I wore today kill my feet."

"Then why do you wear them?" he persisted.

Because they make my ass look good, and my legs look less stumpy.

"Because they matched my outfit," I lied.

He made a sound of amusement in his throat, and I shifted again, feeling the stirring of arousal once again hit me.

God, I wanted the man more than anything.

"I never understood the appeal," he murmured. "When I went pro for that first year, they forced us to wear suits and shit. The shoes were the worst. I swear to Christ, I dreaded game days just because I'd be forced into them."

I smiled, which was followed shortly after by a shiver as the building around us started to shake.

I swallowed as fear started to clog my throat.

"Swear to God," I murmured, seemingly to myself. "I never wanted to die a virgin."

Everything froze.

His breathing. My breathing. The pounding rain and the ear-piercing wind.

Hell, I couldn't even hear the tornado sirens anymore.

What was meant to come out barely a whisper sounded like an atomic bomb being dropped in the middle of Ezra's miniscule bathroom.

I squeezed my eyes tightly shut and started to count down from twenty in my head.

I wanted to bang my head against the tiled wall behind my head to beat some sense into my godforsaken brain.

Only, before I could do that, Ezra's hands were on my hips, hauling me over the top of him.

I gasped, surprised at the sudden movement.

Then I found his mouth slanting over the top of mine, and shit you not, I orgasmed right then and there.

I felt things inside of me clench, and the fever pitch I'd been at all night went from a slow burn at around a five on the holy shit scale, to a full-on fifteen.

I moaned into his mouth as things in my lower body started to pulse, and my pussy clenched on nothing.

There was no time to gain control of myself, though. Ezra wouldn't let me.

We went from kissing to stripping our clothes off in a matter of seconds.

I don't know what happened after that with the storm, because the storm inside of my body was trumping anything that happened on the outside.

Things started to happen at a fast pace.

First, I became naked before him, mostly because I was on top of him, and he was trying to free his jeans from his hips while I was still firmly planted on top of him.

Second, I might or might not have slammed my head into his chin once or twice on accident.

Last, and this was the most important, I got an eye-full of Ezra's penis.

"Jesus Christ," I breathed.

My gaze turned to the side, and I stared at his cock's—which was sticking straight up and pointing at the ceiling—shadow. With the candle positioned as it was, his penis, as well as both of our bodies, were silhouetted along the wall to our left.

And the thing looked bigger than life.

I held up my arm in comparison and swallowed.

That was when he started to laugh.

"Jesus Christ, you make a man feel good," he murmured.

Then he was running the tip of one finger along the tan areola of my left breast.

I looked at him, and his eyes were hot and captivated—by me.

"You're really big," I accused.

His eyes lifted to mine.

"You're holding your arm about four inches from my cock. Of course, it's going to look big in shadow," he teased.

I looked down at the real thing and shook my head. "No. It's *big*."

I'd never been this close to a penis before.

In fact, all that excitement that was running through my veins just a scant minute before was now gone. In that excitement's place was trepidation.

I wanted this. I wanted this so bad I could practically taste it.

But I was not an experienced woman. In fact, I'd literally only had one single kiss by a boy in college. That was it.

Everything was new to me, and that included all things that had to do with big equipment—i.e., penises.

His finger started to trail away from the areola and circled closer and closer to the tip of my breast until suddenly he had my nipple between two fingers.

I gasped when he pinched it. Startled, I looked up in surprise.

"You can take me."

It wasn't a statement as much as an order.

And when the thunder boomed outside, followed by a weird whistling noise, I said the first thing to come to my mind.

"If the walls come down around us, we're going to be naked," I told him. "And when rescuers come looking for us, they'll find everything hanging out. Think of the children."

That was when Ezra McDuff lost his patience.

He launched himself forward until my entire body was plastered to his, and he started to feast on me.

His mouth went to my breast, latching on like a man starved for touch. His hands went to my ass, and he pressed down, urging me to feel his erection pinned between my body and his.

And oh, sweet baby Jesus. The man had such a sweet mouth.

I gasped and latched onto his shoulders, fingernails digging into the soft skin at the top of his back.

I was sure that I was hurting him, but he didn't stop his assault on my nipple, nor did he let up the pressure on my ass, allowing me to grind down into him while also trying to figure out what to do next.

Should I stay where I was? Should I move my hands? Should I touch him?

All the thoughts swirling in my mind was enough to frustrate me, but before it could get to the point where I made an awkward attempt at seduction, he moved so that I was on my back, and he was over me.

I gasped, surprised by the lightning fast move.

But that was as fast as he got. The moment he had me where he wanted me, he slowed down to an almost sloth-like pace.

His mouth was everywhere, though.

On my breast, trailing up the middle of my chest, sucking on my collarbone. On the curve of my mouth.

I groaned and thrust my hands into his hair, needing something, anything to hold onto.

He growled as I pulled, but he didn't stop me.

Oh, no.

Not Ezra.

Apparently, he enjoyed the sting of pain. I knew that not because of his body language, or his sign of satisfaction, but because of his mouth opening and him flat out telling me.

"Yes," he hissed. "Put your legs around my hips, grind your pussy up into me while you pull my hair."

And suddenly, just like that, I felt like I could do this.

The nerves were gone.

The insecurity, and the fear.

I did exactly as he instructed, wrapping my legs around his trim waist, and lifting myself up to tease him with my pussy.

His hard, hot cock slid in between my pussy lips, and he started to rock back and forth, coating the length of his dick in my excitement.

"Do you want my cock, Raleigh?" he teased.

Did I want his cock? Did he think I was stupid? Of course, I wanted it!

"Yes," I breathed. "I want you inside of me."

He shifted so that his cock was rubbing deliciously over every square inch of my lips.

"Are you on birth control?"

I nodded, swallowing hard. "Yes."

The timid word was met with a groan of approval.

"I've wanted this for a long time," he rasped against my throat, reaching one hand down to pluck at my distended nipple.

Not as long as I have, I thought morosely.

A boom of thunder sounded overhead, followed shortly by a crack of something falling outside.

But I didn't care—couldn't care—because I felt his cock pull back through my folds, and then get lodged at the entrance of my pussy.

I opened my eyes, wanting to see his face when he entered me and got rewarded with his eyes pinned to mine.

"Ready, baby?" he questioned.

I nodded, my throat too full of excitement to speak.

He started to push, and my entrance promptly protested.

"Reach between us with both hands and spread your pussy lips," he ordered.

Biting my lip, I reluctantly let go of his hair and slid my hands down between our abdomens, not missing the fact that everywhere my touch had been goosebumps followed.

The minute I got to where we were connected, I had a sudden burst of adrenaline shoot through me.

We were about to do this.

I was about to have Ezra McDuff's big penis inside of me.

Holy. *Shit.*

I pulled my pussy lips apart, and he sank a quarter inch inside, causing us both to freeze.

Something momentous passed in between us then, but before either one of us could examine it for more than a few seconds, my pussy rippled around what little he had inside of me, causing him to groan.

With his eyes still connected with mine, he pushed inside.

I'd expected pain, but there wasn't any.

Discomfort, yes. Pain, no.

The moment that he started to fill me, other things started to cloud my judgment—like how good he felt with only half of his cock inside of me. Or, possibly it could've been the way he was staring at me so intently that I felt not only stripped physically bare but mentally as well.

I licked my lips, and his gaze moved down to my mouth.

After a short hesitation, his arms bulged as he came down, being sure to put almost zero pressure on me, keeping every bit of his weight on his arms, he kissed me.

He kissed me so thoroughly that when he finally let me up for air, I was gasping for breath, which was just as well seeing as while I was temporarily distracted, he thrust forward and gave me every single bit of his length.

The cry of pleasure that left me almost boneless left my throat, and soon I felt his balls pressed up against my ass.

Our breathing was ragged, but mostly it was the way my chest was puffing like a freight train that had his gaze shifting from excitement to worry.

"Are you okay?" he murmured, lips brushing my cheek.

I nodded, loving the way his whiskers rubbed against my cheek. "More than okay…if you'd only move."

He chuckled, pulling his hips back slightly, only to thrust back forward again, filling me before I could truly miss his departure.

"You feel like heaven wrapped around me." He ran one finger from my chest up to my hair, burying his fist in the now-knotted strands.

Another boom of thunder shook our small hideout, but that didn't stop him from moving into a rhythm.

Both of us were cramped. My head was up against the soap holder, and I could see his leg extended out beyond the back of the toilet, but neither one of us seemed to care.

Not when he felt so fucking good inside of me, and definitely not when I had the one and only thing I'd ever wanted in my arms.

"God, I'm not going to last," he rasped against my throat.

His hand shifted to go between us, the pad of his thumb easily finding that bundle of nerves I'd only ever touched in the darkness of my own locked bedroom.

The moment he made contact with the small nub, everything inside of me clenched with need and anticipation.

It wouldn't take much for him to make me fall over the edge— something that surprised me since when I did this myself, it took quite a long time for me to let go.

Ezra didn't seem to have that same problem.

"Please be close," he groaned into my neck, moving his hand away. "Get yourself off."

My hand moved.

I was, but that close turned into falling overboard when he bit my neck with blunt teeth.

The dual sensations had me losing every ounce of control I'd managed to hold onto.

My pussy clamped down around him, and moments later, I was screaming my head off—and it had absolutely nothing to do with the window outside breaking, and everything to do with Ezra's cock.

Between one scream and the next, I was coming so hard that if it wasn't storming, I was sure that the neighbors would've come over to check to make sure I was okay.

I'd never, not once in my life, felt something so ferocious sweep through my body.

My eyes slammed shut, my connection to Ezra's beautiful gaze falling to the wayside. My legs clamped even tighter around his hips, and my arms froze. One in his hair, and the other on my clit.

Ezra's curse of agony followed mine, and had I heard it any other time when I wasn't experiencing my out of body experience, I would've definitely asked him if he was okay.

Turns out, he was dying his own little death, but I was too lost to care.

At least not until long moments later, when the wind died down, and our breathing started to calm.

"You know," he murmured, sounding almost disappointed in himself. "I've taught that sex-ed class for years. I've blasted the safe sex point home more times than I can count, and then bam. You walk into my life, and I lose every single bit of self-control I thought I had."

I didn't know what to say to that.

"I'm clean," I breathed against his chest.

He snorted. "Honey, your virginity is staining my still hard dick right now. I have no doubt in my mind that you're clean."

I felt my lips twitch.

I couldn't really say what I was thinking, because what I was thinking probably wasn't something he needed to hear.

Because if I told him that the idea of having his baby was overtly appealing to me, and I hoped that he'd gotten me pregnant, he might very well realize how crazy I was, and kick me out.

Therefore, I kept my mouth shut and tried not to act excited about having sex with Ezra McDuff—my high school crush, and Ezra losing so much control that he forgot the number one rule of sex— glove it if you love it.

Lani Lynn Vale

CHAPTER 8

Eating is cheaper than therapy.

-Fact of Life

Ezra

My anger at my team had not abated despite having a three-day weekend to calm down.

Then again, seeing the fields that I'd painstakingly worked so hard on trashed due to the weather a few days ago hadn't helped matters, either.

Honestly, the only thing saving these kids from having to run for the next three weeks straight was the looseness that I felt after spending the night with Raleigh.

When I walked onto the field Tuesday afternoon, every single boy looked bored to tears.

They didn't seem scared. They didn't look particularly ashamed. They looked like they were ready to hang out and play some recreational ball.

Well, I was sorry to say, they wouldn't be playing ball at all today.

They'd be running.

And when they weren't running, they'd be doing burpees.

Two of the most awful things I could think of.

"Let's head to the track," I ordered, waving my hand in the direction of where I wanted them to go.

Groans filled the air.

"What for, Coach?"

I looked over my shoulder at my nephew.

"Unfortunately, a few ruined it for you all. Since you're all a team, you will be punished as a team." I paused. "And next time you see your teammates doing something stupid, you will say something to help convince them of why it's not a good idea."

Another round of groans.

"Come on, Coach. It wasn't that big of a deal."

I froze when I heard Mackie's rebuttal.

"Not that big of a deal?" I turned to look at him. "Tell me, how the hell do you think it's not that big of a deal? You laughed at a boy that lost everything. *Everything*, Mackie."

The boys shuffled on their feet, clearly rethinking their actions from three nights before.

"Riggs," I called out, pointing at the shortstop. "What would you do if you couldn't walk anymore?"

Riggs didn't say a word.

"And you, Boney," I called, pointing at my relief pitcher. "What would you do if you woke up one day and realized that you couldn't get yourself to the toilet to take a shit?"

Still nothing.

"Jacks." I looked at the catcher who standing next to me. "What would you do if you found out that you could never drive that shiny new truck again?"

Slowly but surely, I went through each and every senior on the team.

"What would you do if you woke up tomorrow and realized your entire life was over?" I asked. "That you had to relearn the basics. Figure out how to do things that you had mastered when you were a baby? How to eat. How to sleep. How to get to the bathroom. How to shower. How to do just about everything you've always taken for granted."

"Shit."

That came from Riggs.

"Y'all know as well as I do that Morgan's life was baseball," I continued. "How do you think it makes him feel to know that you don't support him?"

Every single boy looked at their feet, but I had a feeling that the little shit Mackie only did it because he didn't want to be out of place amongst the group.

If Mackie wasn't such a good player, I'd think about kicking him off the team.

He was a selfish prick and I'd honestly never come as close as I did with Mackie to hating a student.

My anger rose once again, and I narrowed my eyes at the entire team.

"Unfortunately for you underclassmen, y'all are going to share in the seniors' punishment." I paused to look at my nephew, giving him an annoyed glance. Once my eyes were turned back to the group of seniors, I let them hear the anger in my voice. "I may not be able to physically touch you, but I can still kick your ass. Now run."

***

Raleigh

I looked up, startled to find fifteen sweaty boys standing in my way.

I swallowed, trying not to relay my fears of having all of them standing there, blocking my way out.

"We came to apologize." Johnson looked apologetic.

All of them did. All of them but a few. But those few were outnumbered by the rest that did.

One face, in particular, Mackie Tombs, stood out. And not in a good way. I had a feeling that if these other boys weren't there with him, he might very well be doing the opposite of apologizing.

"Um, thank you?" I replied hesitantly.

Johnson's lips twitched, and he shook his head, causing his shaggy hair to fall haphazardly over his face.

Bolstering my courage by looking at his face, I turned to the other boys, one by one, and looked each of them in the eyes.

"I realize that y'all think it's a joke." I paused. "But this bullying stuff is serious business. You don't know anything about a person that you're bullying. You have no idea what's going on at home. You don't know whether his father just died, or his entire life had changed due to a parent losing a job. Of course, in Morgan's case, you do know some of what he's facing…but you also don't know the struggle that he's going through. Y'all should be role models, not bullies."

Feet shuffled, and I smiled then. "I appreciate y'all coming over to apologize. But I think that Morgan could use the apologies more

112

than I could…and I also think it wouldn't hurt you to spend a little time with your friend. I'm sure that he misses y'all."

Morgan didn't have any friends any longer. It was like he'd isolated himself, doing what he could to put up a shield and keep people that wanted to be his friend out.

Murmurs of agreement filled the air, and all of a sudden, I realized that these boys had no idea that Morgan missed them.

"All right, guys." I smiled softly at them. "Y'all should probably head home and get showered…don't y'all have a test in sexual education coming up tomorrow?"

Chuckles filled the air, but again, Mackie only glared.

I swallowed and looked away from his gaze.

Moments after issuing the dismissal, they all left, leaving me staring at their retreating backs.

Biting my lip, I started down the walkway leading to the parking lot about fifteen steps behind them, being sure to keep enough distance in between me and them to be sure I felt safe.

I'd learned my triggers, and since one of them was being too close to a group of boys, I kept my distance.

I'd just rounded the final corner to the parking lot when I realized that Mackie was holding back. He was at least eight to ten paces behind the rest of the team, and Johnson was looking over his shoulder every couple of steps to keep an eye on him.

I felt my heart warm, loving that he was protective like his father—and his uncle.

His uncle that I hadn't seen nor spoken to in well over forty-eight hours.

At first, I'd beaten myself up about it. Told myself that he was having second thoughts about what we'd done. Then I realized that the cell towers were out due to the weather we'd had roll through, and he didn't know where I lived.

And this morning, all hands had been on deck when it came to helping clean up around the school, meaning I hadn't seen him there, either.

Hell, I was honestly surprised we were even at school today since we didn't have power in all of the buildings.

The cafeteria ovens and microwaves were being run off of generators, and luckily it was spring, meaning it wasn't oppressively hot.

And, if I was a guessing girl, I would say that today had been more productive than other days because there was nothing to inhibit the children from learning. There were no cell phones out, or disturbing influences. I'd taken almost all of my classes outdoors so we could do work in the sun—and I had to say, my kids in every class had given me better work than I'd had from them all school year.

"Yo," Johnson called, startling me. "Is something wrong, Mackie?"

I looked up to find Mackie way closer to me than to the rest of the group, causing me to slow my pace.

Johnson along with a few other players stopped as well and hung back until Mackie was back in line with them again.

I felt a sense of relief wash over me as Johnson hung back to walk with me.

"Hello, Johnson," I called softly. "Have you seen your uncle lately?"

He gave me a droll look. "Before or after he kicked our asses during practice?"

I felt my lips twitch.

"Uhhh," I hesitated. "Was it bad?"

"We ran two miles, then did a thousand burpees. Do you know how long that took us?" He paused, looking at me with a sense of exhaustion about him.

I was scared to ask what a burpee was.

But I did it anyway.

He looked at me like I'd lost my mind. "You don't know what a burpee is?"

I shook my head.

Then he surprised the ever-loving crap out of me by dropping into a push-up position on the ground, doing a push-up, then snapping up into a squat position before jumping in the air.

"That," he winced, "is a burpee. You're lucky I was able to get up from doing it. I burned a thousand and two calories during that workout. That means I can have four hamburgers for dinner and it won't matter."

I laughed, which was when I looked up and spotted Ezra leaning against my car.

I also spotted Mackie's glare over his shoulder moments after that that wiped the smile straight off my face.

A shiver slid down my spine, and I wondered what it was that I'd ever done to the kid.

I'd never sent him to the principal, and I'd never said a word to him except to call his name on the roster during our sex-ed class to make sure he was in attendance.

I groaned inwardly.

"Bye, Uncle Ezra," Johnson called as he passed. "Don't do anything I wouldn't do."

Ezra snorted. "Says the person that does stupid shit all the freakin' time."

He flipped Ezra off before walking to Ezra's truck that had a crack in the windshield—just like mine did—only on a much smaller scale.

As we'd left the night of the storm, it became apparent quickly that the loud bang we'd heard outside of Ezra's bathroom window had been a tree limb falling down on top of Ezra's truck.

That'd been nothing compared to mine—which was a metal sign falling from the bleachers above where my car had been parked, impaling it.

In fact, the metal sign was still there because neither Ezra nor I could get it out. Though Ezra did manage to cut the majority of the pole off the sign.

He'd tried to take me home, but I'd refused, saying my car was perfectly functional.

He'd reluctantly agreed since Grady had been repairing damage to their garage as we'd been leaving.

The impaled sign was on the very right side of my windshield, completely out of my viewing space, and the only thing, cosmetically, wrong with the entire windshield. There weren't even any cracks branching off of the impaled object.

Tomorrow I'd be taking it to a body shop, but until then, I was stuck with it.

The funny thing was, the sign said 'violators will be towed.'

I felt a blush hit my face the moment that Ezra and I were alone.

He took it in, and immediately grinned as he caught sight of me.

"Hey," I whispered, feeling like I'd swallowed a chili pepper.

Ezra grinned. "Hey yourself. What are you doing here so late?"

I grimaced. "Grading papers and inputting them online. I was going to put it all in last night, but since we didn't have power, I had to do it in the library with about eight other teachers trying to accomplish the same thing. Luckily, the cafeteria loaned out their generator for the night."

Ezra grunted. "The power company estimates the power being back on tomorrow morning." He looked at me, letting his eyes trail lazily down my body. "Are you busy? Do you want to get some dinner with me?"

I felt butterflies take flight in my belly.

"I...can't," I whispered. "I made arrangements to have dinner with my folks tonight because I still don't have power. You're more than welcome to go with me."

He blinked. Then he grinned. "I wouldn't mind. We don't have power, either."

It was my turn to blink then.

"You...wouldn't mind?" I asked, flabbergasted. "Are you sure? My family is pretty crazy."

Crazy didn't even begin to cover it.

Ezra chuckled. "Have you met mine?"

I didn't reply. "You know where they live?"

He nodded.

"You can meet me there at six. I have to go home and change first, or my mother will bitch and complain that I'm trying to ruin my work clothes as if she was still the one paying for them—which she's not," I hurried to add.

"How about we both go change, and I pick you up at your place at five forty-five?" he offered.

I licked my suddenly dry lips. "I'd like that."

It was only when I was halfway home that I realized he'd never asked where I lived.

I wasn't sure if that was a good thing or a bad thing.

Ezra was intense. Him knowing where to find me almost sent me into a panic attack.

Not because I didn't want him to find me…but because I did.

CHAPTER 9

I'm not trying to be difficult. It just comes naturally.

-Text from Raleigh to Ezra

Ezra

Raleigh and I arrived at five minutes to six, and the look on her parents' faces was enough to make me want to laugh.

But I didn't.

Instead, I offered my hand to Mr. Crusie, followed shortly by Ms. Crusie.

Apparently, they knew exactly who I was, even though I didn't know them—at least not as well as they knew me.

I'd, of course, seen them around town. Other than a 'hello, how are you,' I really hadn't had much interaction with either of them.

"Mother," Raleigh hissed. "Seriously, stop staring at him like you want to munch on his Cheerios."

"Whose Cheerios are we wanting to munch on?" A man about ten years older than me pulled the door open. "What the fuck are you doing here?"

"Croft!" Ms. Crusie snarled, slapping Croft, who I assumed was Raleigh's brother, on the stomach.

He '*ooofed*' as he doubled over and sent his mother a glare. "What was that for?"

"You know exactly what that was for, Croft Crusie," she snapped. "Go inside before I kick your ass."

I bit my lip to keep my laugh inside.

Raleigh didn't have the same compunction. She bent over, holding her stomach and started to wheeze as she attempted to say between guffaws, "She'll kick your ass. Watch out, Croft. Momma's gonna kick yo' ass!"

"That ass kicking doesn't stop with boys, darlin'," Ms. Crusie explained darkly. "Keep sayin' ass and find out where it gets you."

Raleigh stood straight, wiping away tears, a full smile still taking up the majority of her face.

Her eyes were on her mom, but mine were on her.

She was beautiful. How had I missed this for so long?

I felt like a dumbass. A really big, clueless dumbass that didn't know what was right in front of his face until it hit him square in the jaw.

"Let's go inside," Mr. Crusie suggested. "And you can call me Gates. This is Merida."

I nodded and followed them all inside, blinking momentarily at the décor.

"Umm," I hesitated. "Well, I'm guessing you like chickens?"

Gates murmured, "Merida *loves* chickens. There's a difference."

"Oh, hush." Merida sighed. "It's not a bad thing to love chickens. And it's certainly not a bad thing to want more."

"You have over fifty...and we're in the city. Trust me when I say that we're gonna get busted one day for havin' them, and when we do, you're gonna have to get rid of them."

Merida shook her head. "We'd move before I allowed that to happen."

I had no doubt in my mind that she would if push came to shove.

"What kinds of chickens?" I asked. "My sister wants a Polish. The ones with the crazy hair."

I put my hand up over my head, mimicking the way that the feathers were on the top of a Polish's head.

Merida laughed, and Raleigh looked at me like I'd just broken through some imaginary wall I hadn't known was erected.

She wanted me to like her parents...and she was happy that they liked me back.

Well, her mom did anyway. Her father and Croft were still up for debate.

"Honey." Merida took her daughter's hand. "Help me serve up dinner. Boys, y'all go get the drinks that you want from the garage and then meet at the table. Got it? Good."

She left before any of us nodded our consent, and we were all left staring at each other, a little dumbfounded at her sudden departure.

"Now!" Merida called from somewhere beyond the living room we were standing in—my guess was the kitchen.

Raleigh sighed, looking between me and her brother, then to her father, and back again.

"Don't do anything stupid." Raleigh looked first at her father, then to her brother.

With that, she left, leaving me alone with two men who didn't look anywhere near as accepting of me as they'd been when Raleigh had been standing there.

"So…" Croft started. "You finally decided to give her the time of day?"

I tilted my head. "I what?"

His eyes narrowed, and he opened his mouth to say something before Gates slammed his hand on Croft's shoulder.

Just when I was about to ask 'what' a second time, Camryn, another teacher from the school that Raleigh and I worked at, came bustling in, a frazzled look on her face.

"Hi, Gates. Douche. Ezra," Camryn said on her way past.

I followed her whirlwind, then turned to face 'douche.'

"Douche?" I asked carefully.

Gates started to laugh. "Seems my children suck at seeing what's right in front of their eyes."

With that cryptic statement, Gates walked away calling out for me to follow. "Come on. I have good beer."

I followed, because who the hell wouldn't want good beer? Especially amongst this crowd.

It was two hours later, when dinner was consumed, and I was forced to the back porch with Croft and Gates once again, when it happened.

Camryn, who I learned was Raleigh's best friend, and Merida, along with Raleigh, were in the kitchen cleaning dishes, then bringing dessert out.

I, on the other hand, was outside even though I wanted to be inside to help them clean. But, when I'd made that attempt, Raleigh had shaken her head and ushered me into the back yard, which was where I now found myself.

"So…how did you and my baby sister start being a thing?" Croft questioned.

I shrugged. "I saw her a bit at school this year, and she took over my sex-ed class…"

"She took over your sex-ed class?" Croft's voice rose. "Isn't that a seniors' class?"

I nodded. "Yeah. How'd you know?"

"Same high school, bro. And I'm not that old." He paused. "But Raleigh doesn't teach seniors. That was the agreement."

I didn't have any idea what he was speaking of. "Agreement?"

"Yeah," he looked at me. "When Raleigh started working for Gun Barrel ISD, part of the agreement when she signed on was that she wouldn't be assigned any age levels over freshman." He looked at me like I was crazy. "I don't…why would they do that to her knowing that she has panic attacks?"

My stomach dropped. "Panic attacks?"

I'd heard nothing of any panic attacks. Not from the principal that I'd addressed it with to find help with my class, and not from Raleigh.

"Yeah. When she was attacked while being a student teacher during her schooling, she suffered some PTSD. Now, any time she gets close to the bigger boys, she kind of freezes up. Hyperventilates. That's why we're really careful about her being at sporting events. If she does go, one of us is always with her."

I felt bile rising up the back of my throat.

"I don't…I don't know what you're talking about," I admitted. "She never…"

The sheer horror of what he was insinuating made me want to vomit.

"She never told you," Gates supplied, sounding just as miffed as Croft.

And, if what I was understanding was true, he had a reason to be.

The more I sat there and thought about it, the more that it made sense.

A sick sort of sense that made me want to throw up the good food I'd just consumed.

"Shit," I said, running my hands through my hair. "She told me that she was okay with it."

"More like, she told you what everyone wanted to hear," Croft grumbled. "What do you want to bet that they threatened her job?"

I didn't want to know. I didn't want to be partially responsible for what she'd gone through, either.

I closed my eyes. "What happened?"

That was when the two men took ten painstaking minutes to explain what had happened to Raleigh, and why she was the way she was.

And now everything became clear.

Why she became antsy when she was around the baseball team. Why she avoided sporting games—because most of them were with large, rowdy boys that were the very thing that scared her.

And, to make matters worse, she'd been terrified to do a class with seniors, and I'd been the one to make it happen.

"Fuck," I groaned.

Before we could talk any more about it, though, the door opened and Camryn walked out, followed shortly by Merida.

Raleigh was the last one out, and she smiled at me as she took a step over the threshold.

In her hand was a bottle of beer for me, and a can of Dr. Pepper for her.

She'd just made it to where she was reaching back for the doorknob when she tripped on air and went flying.

I saw what was about to happen about two seconds before it actually did, but I could do nothing to stop it.

She went down face first.

The bottle of beer fell with a crash against the concrete, and she landed directly on top of it.

We were all up and out of our chairs, and I was lifting Raleigh to her feet, when we saw the blood.

"Shit," Raleigh whined. "I was supposed to run tomorrow!"

"Raleigh," her father said, sounding amused. "You don't run."

I bit my lip and reached for a beach towel that'd been resting along the back of the chair I'd taken up residence in and pressed it against her bleeding thigh—perilously close to other more pleasant things.

She blushed profusely when my big hand got close to other parts of her anatomy, but she didn't complain or pull away.

"I was going to go run with Ezra," she explained. "But this is going to need stitches."

I pulled the towel away from her leg and nodded my head.

She was going to need stitches.

Shit.

"Not it," Camryn, Croft, and Gates said at the same time.

Merida sighed. "Y'all suck."

Raleigh scowled.

"What?" I asked her, likely sounding confused. "Does it hurt?"

She shrugged. "It doesn't feel all that great, no. But that wasn't what I was grimacing about."

"Then what were you grimacing about?" I asked.

She gestured to the group at her back.

Merida was already heading inside.

She came back moments later with her purse slung over her shoulder and an impatient look on her face.

"I'll take her," I said, standing up. "Hold that there so you don't lose half your body weight in blood."

She was so freakin' small that it wouldn't take much for her to get to the point where she was woozy, that was for sure.

Merida beamed at me. "We normally take her to the doc in town. We'll give him a call and tell him that you're on the way."

With that, they practically ushered us out of their house.

Moments later, when we were safely in the truck, I looked over at Raleigh, who didn't look amused.

"Do they always do that?" I wondered as I started the truck up.

Raleigh shrugged. "I get hurt a lot. I go to the doctor at least twice a year for doing stupid things like I just did. It's understandable that they don't want to take me."

I didn't agree.

But that was just me.

If she was ever in need, it'd never get old taking care of her.

The more I got to know the woman by my side, the more I realized what a fool I'd been for not paying attention to her.

"Where to, darlin'?" I purred.

She narrowed her eyes on me. "You can just take me home. I'll drive myself. This really isn't a big deal, I promise."

I ignored her promise and headed into town, grinning widely when she sighed deeply in the seat next to me.

When she didn't look at me for the next ten minutes, I'd thought it was due to me not taking her home so she could drive herself.

Turns out, as we pulled into the parking lot of the one and only clinic in town, it was due to the fact that she was embarrassed that I'd witnessed yet another faux pas on her part.

"Listen." She turned in the seat and looked at me. "I'm a mess. I have accidents happen every day. I'm scared of the dark. I trip over air. I break at least one bone a year, and honestly? I'm not really sure why you're even still with me."

My brow rose at her admission.

"And you're deathly afraid of working with seniors," I started, watching her eyes go wide.

The stillness of her body had her father and brother's points hammered home. She was deathly afraid. She'd also been victimized, and the last nail was hammered home.

"H-how did you know that?" She licked her lips, drawing my attention to that succulent mouth of hers. That mouth I hadn't tasted in well over three days, and it was driving me wild.

"Your brother let it slip that you didn't work with the older age groups. I let it slip that you'd been taking over my sex-ed class." I paused. "And it all degraded from there."

She looked down at her hand, which was holding the bloody towel into place.

"I want to get better…and I'd also like to keep my job. I took it as a sign that this was my time," she explained hesitantly.

I didn't know what to say to that.

On one hand, I completely agreed with her. She needed to get over her fear. It wasn't healthy.

But I also didn't want her to ever be scared in the first place—no matter what the cause.

"They wouldn't have fired you," I promised. "I wouldn't have let them."

She laughed. "You didn't even know me then, Ezra. I was still invisible."

I winced. "I would've known that you were fired because you didn't take over my class. I wouldn't have stood for it."

She smiled sadly.

"Well, it's not like you need to worry about it anymore. I'm perfectly fine, and I'm working through my fears." She paused. "And your class is full of boys that are sweet. The girls are even sweeter. I'm lucky."

"Next year you might not be," I admitted. "What then?"

She sighed. "Next year it might not matter because I might be hit by a random bus crossing the road, and I'll no longer be of this planet."

Her flippancy made me angry.

"Don't."

Her eyes widened. "Don't what?"

"Don't joke," I said. "Not about that."

The idea of her not being around anymore felt like a blow right to the heart.

I hadn't realized how attached I'd become until tonight. Her sweetness. Her beauty. Her teasing. Not having it around me anymore scared the absolute crap out of me, which in turn terrified me even more at the intensity of my feelings for her.

I'd never felt like this before. This feeling was utterly new, and it felt like something that was making my heart feel like it might burst straight the fuck out of my chest.

"Let's go," I ordered, getting out of my seat. "I don't want that getting infected."

She laughed. "Isn't alcohol a disinfectant?"

I gave her a roll of my eyes. "Sure, let's go with that."

Teasingly, she flipped me off, but the lightness and laughter shining in her eyes was much better than seeing the terror of moments before as we spoke about what had happened to her.

Needless to say, I'd do just about anything to see her smile.

Lani Lynn Vale

CHAPTER 10

It's lit.

-Thomas Edison

Raleigh

I got six stitches in my thigh and a shot in the ass due to my clumsiness.

The icing on the cake was Ezra watching me bend over and pull down my pants, a look of heat in his eyes.

Now, I was sitting in the front seat of his truck in front of my house, wondering if I could talk him into coming inside.

Unfortunately, I knew that the moment he walked around the hood of the truck and helped me out that he wasn't going to stay. Even if I asked nicely.

He looked shaken after what he'd learned about my assault and hadn't gotten rid of the look ever since my dad and Croft had told him about it.

To make matters worse, he'd literally watched me get stitches with horror written all over his face.

Which then, in turn, made me feel stupid because I'd gone and screwed myself up, showing him exactly what he would be getting if he continued to date me.

And the bad thing was, ever since the night that we'd slept together, he hadn't made a single move in my direction since.

He hadn't even tried to cop a feel or kiss me.

Hugs, yes—not that I was complaining about Ezra hugs, they were the best—but there were other things I liked about him, too. Such as his lips…and his penis.

Like right now, he was keeping so much distance between us that I could definitely not miss the signs.

I was making him nervous.

"Do you want to come inside?" I asked, trying not to sound hopeful.

He shook his head. "I have an early morning practice tomorrow."

I looked down at my feet. "I guess I'll see you at the staff meeting tomorrow?"

I sounded almost hopeful as I asked that, and I knew that I likely sounded pathetic, too.

"I'll be there." He grinned, gesturing for me to walk to the door. "Thank you for inviting me to your parents' place."

I shrugged. "I'm not sure that I was actually the one to invite you…"

He chuckled and stopped at the bottom step, while I continued up the other three steps that led to my front porch.

Once the door was open, I flipped the porch light on and then turned to stare down at the man I'd never once entertained the possibility of being at my house.

Let alone dropping me off.

I guess I should be happy that he'd actually noticed me.

Yet…I wasn't.

At least not any longer.

I was obsessed with the man, and I wanted so much more it wasn't even funny.

"Well," I hesitated, sounding nervous. "Be careful on the way home."

Ezra winked and then started to back down the pathway back to my driveway.

"I'll see you tomorrow."

I looked down at my hands, away from that perfect smile so I wouldn't launch myself at him. When I next looked up, he was at his truck and climbing inside.

When he sat there watching me expectantly, I frowned.

He gestured with his chin, and I looked over my shoulder to see the opened door at my back.

I frowned.

"What?" I mouthed, seeing no need to actually say the words since he wouldn't be able to hear them anyway.

Go. Inside.

He mouthed those words back at me, and I chafed inwardly.

Turning my back on the man of my dreams, I walked inside and shut the door before locking it tightly.

Once that was done, only then did I hear the roar of his truck start up.

Hurrying to the window, I looked outside and watched him back down my driveway, and then accelerate down the street.

Sighing in defeat, I flipped the lights back out, and then hurried to my bedroom.

After stripping off my beer and blood-stained pants, I walked to the shower and hosed myself off, hating that I had to wash the scent of Ezra off my skin.

Moments after getting out, I heard my phone ringing from my pants pocket where I'd left it, and hurried to it, putting it to my ear before I'd even looked at who was calling.

I smiled when I heard his voice, but frowned moments after that when I realized that he hadn't meant to call me.

Had he meant to call me, he most assuredly wouldn't have called me while also talking to another woman at the same time.

Ezra was a lot of things, but a mean person wasn't one of them.

And it didn't take a magic 8-ball to see that I cared for him.

"I'm sorry, Ezra," an achingly familiar voice said quietly. "You look rough. Are you sure you don't want to catch a drink?"

Shuffling noises sounded, and then I heard Ezra speak, but I couldn't make out what the words were before the woman's voice started to fill the line again.

"Or we can go get ice cream."

And it was then that I realized that I was definitely a jealous hag.

Ezra and I hadn't made any promises to each other whatsoever. However, whether he realized it or not, I'd given him one.

It was just sad that I would likely never get one from him.

"...Ice cream," I heard Ezra reply.

I frowned, pulling the phone away from my ear, and wondering what I should do.

I, of course, had many options. One major one being hanging up and hoping he didn't butt dial me all over again.

The other option was to listen to what was being said, and not say a word.

I did what any sane woman would do.

I listened.

To every. Freakin'. Word.

"I'm glad that you'll come," I heard Coach Casper say. "I'll see you tomorrow."

My mind went wild as all the possible scenarios went through my brain, and the only logical one I could come up with was the one I kept going back to.

I'd heard Ezra agree to a date with Coach Casper, the one person in the entire school that I'd never get along with.

It was kind of hard to when Coach Casper—I refused to call her by her real name because it was stupid—picked on me all through my informative years.

CHAPTER 11

Eat more hole foods.

-Donut marquee sign

Ezra

"It's a good thing that we get to go home early today," I heard Raleigh say to another teacher, Ms. Holdenbrook. Ms. Holdenbrook was the art teacher and was clearly hanging on Raleigh's every word.

Then again, Ms. Holdenbrook was the third-newest teacher at Gun Barrel ISD, and so new and green that she hadn't even gotten her teaching certificate in the mail.

Lucky for her she was young, and likely wouldn't be too traumatized by her class of students that she'd taken over when the old art teacher—Mrs. Rosemary—had retired after she'd had a major heart attack.

"Why is that?" Ms. Holdenbrook asked.

"Because a few of the kids thought it'd be hilarious to toilet paper my trees," she muttered darkly.

The sweet little woman I'd left on her doorstep last night was gone. In her place was a raving woman who'd much rather geld me than kiss me.

What the hell?

I didn't know what happened between last night and today, but something sure the fuck had.

She was staring at me like I'd run over her dog right in front of her, and I didn't know what the fuck had happened.

I couldn't even ask her what the fuck was wrong because the goddamn auditorium where we were all shoved was filled to the brim with people.

"I'd like to discuss first the morale in the school," Mrs. Sherpa started with, as she fucking did every single time she started a stupid staff meeting.

We had a hundred thousand things to do today as we got ready for the standardized testing we were starting come Monday, and she wanted to bore us to death with student morale.

"Mrs. Sherpa," one of our veteran teachers, Mrs. Golden, interrupted. "I'm going to be quite honest with you. Morale is absolute shit because we're having to teach to this stupid freakin' test and not to what they should be learning. They're being told if they fail, they won't graduate. They're also scared shitless because they should be planning graduation and getting excited about prom, not whether or not they're going to pass this asshole test."

My lips twitched.

She was right.

I never worried about these tests when I was a kid, and I'd had to take them.

Now, students looked at me like they were on the verge of a panic attack on test days. When I took my test, there was no question on whether I would pass it. Nor was there an equation on whether my neighbor or the kid behind me would pass it.

"Ms. Crusie, do you have something to say?" Mrs. Sherpa asked. "I see you over here sinking in your seat."

That was likely due to the fact that I hadn't looked away from her since she arrived and refused to sit next to me.

She kept casting me nervous sideways glances and my dick was twitching each time she bit that goddamn lip.

"Ummm," she hesitated.

"If you don't feel like paying attention, then why are you even attending?" she snapped.

That's when I lost my patience.

"She doesn't want to tell you that morale is a goddamn crap shoot. That it makes you sound seriously out of the loop because you walk these halls just as well as we do. And honestly? With that threatening memo that went out last week about all of our jobs being in jeopardy if we don't score well on the tests, nobody will say anything. Picking on Ms. Crusie because she's too worried to say anything just makes you sound like a bad guy," I interrupted.

Mrs. Sherpa's eyes came to me.

She took a deep breath and straightened her spine. "I'm sorry, Ms. Crusie. I didn't mean to take my bad mood out on you. Coach McDuff is correct." She started to rub at her temples. "And I have noticed that student morale is down. I was hoping we could make a few concessions this week. Does anyone have any ideas on how we could do that?"

Raleigh hesitantly raised her hand.

"They just opened up the splash pad next door," she said softly when the principal nodded at her. "This Friday is early release. We could spend that morning there, then eat pizza next door before returning to school. And since it's still technically on school property, we wouldn't have to obtain permission slips."

The pizza place and the splash pad they'd just built in town was rented property that the school owned. But I could see one problem.

"As good of an idea as that is, we can't do it because there are too many students," I objected.

"We could take them in shifts," Coach Casper interjected from my side. "Coach McDuff and I can…"

I missed whatever else that Coach Casper said.

My eyes were watching Raleigh, so I *didn't* miss the narrowing of her eyes. Nor did I miss the death glare that she sent Coach Casper's way.

I felt my lips twitch.

She may be mad, but she was not indifferent.

Good.

I leaned down farther into my seat and stared straight ahead as the principal discussed the legalities of the trip with the superintendent.

"All right," Mrs. Sherpa replied. "I'll figure out later if that's acceptable. Who wants to give me a rundown on classes this month? Any trouble?"

I was busy watching Raleigh, so I noticed how she didn't say a damn word about my class.

I raised my hand. "Now that baseball season is underway, I'm more than capable of taking my health class back over."

Mrs. Sherpa's eyebrows rose. "You were just saying how nice it was to have the free time to do the field maintenance."

I shrugged. "They hired a new lawn guy that's going to start soon. I no longer need that free period anymore."

Not to mention I didn't want Raleigh to feel uncomfortable.

But did the woman take the gift she was given?

Hell no.

The stubborn little shit.

"I'd like to keep the class if that's all right," Raleigh broke in. "We're getting along great, and I would hate to have to disrupt their learning."

"It's sex-ed," Coach Casper interjected. "They're not going to be upset over Coach McDuff taking over. No offense, but everyone loves Coach McDuff. There's a waiting list to get into his math classes first and second period."

There was that.

But I wished Coach Casper wouldn't try to help…because she wasn't.

Not at all.

Raleigh's eyes narrowed on me, and then Coach Casper. The clench of her jaw had my dick hardening.

"I'm perfectly capable taking over," I offered. "But if Ms. Crusie wants to keep it, that's fine. I was just offering my expertise."

Mrs. Sherpa nodded. "Who was in charge of drinks today?"

Raleigh raised her hand. "I am, but I couldn't carry all eight gallons of tea by myself, so I still have six to go get out of the staff fridge."

Raleigh stood up as Mrs. Sherpa dismissed her, and I stood up as well. "I'll help."

Raleigh's eyes narrowed. Mrs. Sherpa's dismissive wave had me smiling—on the inside anyway.

Following behind Raleigh's practical jog down the auditorium, I found myself grinning ear to ear.

She was like a scared little rabbit.

CHAPTER 12

*Not to brag, but I don't even need to wear camo
to go unnoticed.*

-Raleigh's secret thoughts

Raleigh

I felt like a hunted deer as I practically ran down the center aisle of the auditorium.

I hurried even faster when I chanced a look over my shoulder and found him gaining, despite him not appearing to rush in the least.

Pushing through the auditorium doors, I cursed myself every way that I could muster.

Why had I acted like I cared? Why did I care?

I shouldn't.

My booted heels clicked on the stained concrete floor as my breathing started to accelerate.

I couldn't decide whether I liked that he was following me, all intimidating like, or if I didn't.

I was leaning toward liked it, which was what scared me.

Not with the way he so easily could accept a date by my most hated enemy—though Coach Casper hadn't done anything overtly mean or confrontational. She just had the bad luck to be pretty and also be attracted to the one man that had always been it for me.

It was when I pulled out my master key—the one that unlocked every single door in the school that all teachers had access to besides the principal's office and other administrative offices—that it happened.

The key fell from my hand, and I stopped and bent all in one motion.

That was when the worst possible thing happened.

My pants split.

With Ezra standing not three feet behind me.

Face flaming, I stood up very carefully and willed myself to disappear. For the ground to open up and swallow me whole.

I felt everything inside of me scream in embarrassment as I prayed for all I was worth that the rip wasn't as bad as I feared it was.

I was wrong.

It was worse.

My hand started searching for the rip, and I found it instantly.

It stretched from my belt all the way down the crack of my ass and disappeared into the crease of my legs.

Son. Of. A. Bitch.

I heard Ezra hiss in a breath as I felt his body crowd me, his torso blanketing me from shoulder to mid-thigh.

I blew out a shaky breath when I felt his erection press against me.

"Can't say I'm too upset," he breathed. "That was the hottest thing I've seen all day."

"W-what?" I stuttered.

He wedged his hand between our bodies and ran the pad of his thumb up and down the bare skin of my ass.

"You're not wearing any panties," he breathed against the back of my head, his breath fanning my hair.

I turned to look up at him.

"I'm wearing panties," I told him. "They're just sheer."

He groaned and looked down into my eyes, and it was then that I saw every single bit of desire that I'd seen that night of the tornado.

He wanted me.

Bad.

Just like I wanted him.

I licked my dry lips, and his eyes followed the movement.

Then he said something that I didn't quite hear.

"What?"

He moved down so that he was even closer to me.

"Better to do this with," he rumbled against my cheek.

Then his hand skidded around my waist and delved down into the gap the tear had created in my jeans.

Moments later, his fingers found my thong and pushed it aside.

I was seconds away from hyperventilating.

And before I could get my wits about me, he started shoving me until I found myself closed in a dark janitor's closet.

I had a second to fear the dark, confined space, and then his mouth was devouring mine.

His hands were down my pants, and I was panting into his mouth while trying to figure out what in the hell I was doing.

"Ezra," I breathed against his wet lips. His soft, plush, bitable lips. "What are you doing?"

"What does it feel like I'm doing?" he asked.

Then he turned me around and yanked my jeans the rest of the way open, making me gasp.

My thong was pushed aside, and I felt the blunt tips of two big fingers testing my readiness.

"Thank God," he growled, sinking both digits inside of me to the webbing of his fingers.

I swallowed a moan, too scared to voice my pleasure in case someone heard, and nearly lost it when he pulled those digits free. I heard him suck each finger clean and then couldn't miss the way his belt buckle clinked.

When I felt the hot ridge of his cock head against my entrance, I didn't resist.

I couldn't…and wouldn't. Not ever.

He was it for me.

He could tell me to drop down on my knees in the middle of the entire teacher body, and I'd do it to please him.

Lucky for me he'd never ask me.

Also lucky for me, he had a dick that made grown women like me scream.

His hand went to my mouth before I could do that, and then his cock was filling me so full that it took everything I had not to come the moment he planted his entire length inside of me.

"Goddamn," I heard him breathe. "You feel so good."

I didn't disagree with him.

He did feel good.

Perfect.

Right.

He thrust into me so hard that I jerked forward, catching myself on the only thing that was there—a shelf filled with cleaning supplies.

Everything—and I do mean everything—went crashing to the floor.

Did Ezra stop fucking me?

Hell no.

He continued, holding on tighter to my hips to keep me from falling.

"So hot and wet," he grunted, flexing his fingers.

I whimpered into my arm, turning my face so that a sound wouldn't escape.

It might as well have not been covered at all—not with the whimpers and sighs escaping.

"Shhhh," he murmured. "Don't talk or they might hear us."

I felt a thrill of anticipation race through me.

That would be a bad thing…wouldn't it?

Being caught fucking in the janitor's closet—the one that I'd heard quite a few people had used before according to the teacher gossip mill—would be humiliating…if Ezra wasn't the one doing the fucking.

Ezra was the town prize—the biggest catch that every single woman in Gun Barrel, Texas was trying to get her hands on. They wanted him for their own, and right now, he was mine. He was inside of me.

And I was about to come.

His thrusts had started out rough, but at some point in our coupling, he'd gained control of himself. His thrusts had become slick, long and exact. He knew exactly what he was doing, and exactly the way to thrust himself inside of me that I got every single inch of his cock playing along those nerve endings I couldn't even reach with my vibrator.

"I'm going to come," I panted. "I'm going to come so hard."

I hadn't even realized that I was saying what I was saying until his hands flexed around my hips, and he lost the rhythm that he'd been taking me with.

His thrusts became erratic, but it didn't matter. I was already *there*.

I came so hard that starbursts filled my eyes, and my lungs seized in my chest.

And then he was coming, too, filling me so full that I'd be wet for the rest of the day.

Thank God today was a teacher in-service day, and we only had to be here half of our usual time.

I had a feeling I'd be leaking *Ezra* from my nether regions until I could get in the shower and rinse him away.

And when he pulled out, I realized that I was downright fucked.

I had no pants to change into, and the rip that'd been there before was now a chasm that would never be mended again.

Oh, and I was wet.

There was that, too.

He rumbled something at me, and I glared at him over my shoulder.

"What am I supposed to do now?" I asked worriedly.

He shrugged. "Well..."

I stood up, feeling the wetness leak out even more, and groaned as I covered my face.

"I can't go back in there looking like this, and I don't have anything to change into since I don't have my car," I whined.

He frowned. "Why don't you have your car?"

I neatly sidestepped that question. "Let me borrow your shirt," I ordered as I snapped my fingers. "I can't walk out there like this."

He looked down at my snapping fingers with a grin on his face, then neatly stuffed himself back in his pants before doing up the zipper.

I watched him with a melancholy expression on my face before I wiped it clean because he was grinning at me in understanding.

I glared and snapped my fingers once again. "Shirt."

He shook his head. "If I give you my shirt, then I won't have one to wear. Do you want me to go in there shirtless? I can offer you some sweatpants, though. I have a pair in my office."

His office was halfway across campus.

"Do you really want me walking practically bare-assed naked through the hall with your stuff dripping out of me?" I questioned.

His eyes heated. "No, but I like the idea of my 'stuff' dripping out of you." Then he pulled me to him and dropped a kiss to my mouth. "I'll walk behind you. Nobody will see, I promise."

I didn't have any other choice but to trust him.

"Fine," I groaned. "But I'm not happy about this."

He winked. "I'm extremely happy. You have no idea."

I wanted to punch him in the throat. "Is that because you accepted a date from Coach Casper last night when you butt dialed me?"

He frowned. "I didn't accept a date from Coach Casper…"

I lifted a brow at him. "You called me, and I heard her ask you out. You said yes. How is that not accepting a date?"

He pulled me close once again, and I had the feeling that he liked that I sounded jealous.

Dammit.

I hadn't meant to let him know how mad I was.

I'd meant to avoid him.

I'd had an epiphany last night, and that was that Ezra McDuff had always been a player, and I wasn't going to tame him.

As much as I liked that he was into me, this couldn't last forever.

I was me, and he was him.

Ezra McDuff was the star football player, and when that football playing status was taken away, he turned into the town's beloved football coach. He was the biggest catch that all of Texas had to offer, since he was offered coaching positions at three of the biggest universities in the country, as well as an assistant coaching position at the professional NFL team in Longview, Texas. And he'd chosen to teach at his hometown high school.

People knew that he was a good man, and women, in general, wanted to make him theirs.

I was just one woman in a long line of women that would likely be only a notch on his bedpost.

"Not a date because I wasn't asked on one. I saw her at the store. She asked me a question about some restaurant. I answered. Then I left." Ezra paused, his voice making my skin tingle. "What are you thinking about so hard up there?"

"Nothing," I lied. "Just hoping that the school doesn't have any hidden cameras that I don't know about."

He snorted. "We'd know about it if they had them. It's an invasion of privacy, and that little thief that keeps stealing all the science lab's supplies would be found already."

I didn't know what he was talking about. "What science lab supplies?"

Ezra stayed right behind me, making sure that I was covered, while also guiding me where he wanted me to go, taking back hallways that I never would've thought to take to get to his office.

"Stuff in the labs is coming up missing. Acid. Beakers. Test tubes. Shit like that. The school board even had a police detective come in and do a little investigating. He wasn't able to find out who it was, either. But we're assuming it's one of the students since ol' Mrs. Hammersmith can barely walk in and out of the school as it is."

"I hadn't heard any of that," I paused. "But then again, nobody but you likes to talk to me anyway."

That didn't sound sad at all, did it?

"I like talking to you," he said. "And Camryn likes talking to you."

I rolled my eyes. "Camryn and I came in at the same time and had the same 'don't talk to me' experience from all the teachers. They looked at us like we were outsiders because we were hired when all of the other teachers were fired the year before due to cut backs."

"I always wondered how you were hired," he offered from behind me as he stopped me before I could pass a non-descript door. "It was kind of odd that we had over ten teachers fired, and then y'all two were hired the following year instead of them hiring back the previous teachers."

I stepped back into him as he bid me to do with his hands on my hips, and he opened the door and pushed me inside the next instant, surprising me.

"Where are w—" He turned on the lights and I was looking at a back way into the gym that I'd never seen before in my life. "Where did this come from?"

Ezra laughed, taking the lead. "It's not used all that often because it leads under the bleachers, and ninety percent of the time the bleachers are closed making this door useless. But since we had a pep rally last week for the baseball game, they were open."

I blinked as I followed behind him, making sure to stay close.

Being under the bleachers always freaked me out, which was why I started to jabber as I practically ran to keep up with him.

"Camryn and I don't know why we were hired," I said. "Apparently, there were just two openings. We both applied and got the jobs. We weren't even aware that the layoffs had happened until we were at the beginning of the year orientation for the staff. Since we'd been away that summer, we literally walked right into chaos. It didn't help that I replaced a teacher that was very loved and adored by not just the faculty, but the student body as well."

Ezra grunted. "Mrs. Peabody was a bitch. She was liked by everyone because she didn't teach her class, and always had students passing her classes because she was too lazy to actually teach like she was supposed to. I used to share classrooms with her. Trust me when I say we are better off now that she's gone."

I'd heard that, too. At least by a few other people that were on the outs with the rest of the staff like I was.

"Camryn is hard not to like, though," I said. "Consequently, when she puts her mind to something, she fits in. Me, on the other hand? I've been here for years now, and I still don't feel like I belong."

And then he was pulling me into his office and shutting the door.

I looked around curiously, spying all the pictures of his family on the desk across the room. One of Moira and him caught my eye, and I smiled. "She doesn't look happy with you, Ezra."

Ezra followed my gaze to the picture and grinned. "Moira likes catching fish, but not touching them."

In the picture, Ezra was holding the fish out to Moira, and Moira was full out screaming her head off.

The one beside it caught my eye, too, and I grimaced.

It was the coaching staff at Gun Barrel High School, and none other than Coach Casper was directly next to Ezra, holding on to him like they were best friends—or lovers.

I looked away. "Where are these sweatpants?"

Ezra walked to a drawer and pulled out a pair of sweats, then tossed them in my direction.

I contemplated looking for a bathroom for all of ten seconds before I shrugged and toed off my shoes, nearly falling over when one caught on my heel and knocked me off balance.

I caught myself on the corner of Ezra's desk and cursed when his cup of pencils and pens fell down and scattered. "Oops."

He chuckled, and I took that as a good sign that he wasn't frustrated with my inability to be a normal person.

At least for now.

Eventually he'd get tired of my annoying ways and move on, just like every single man that showed even an iota of interest in me did.

Once I had my shoes off, I tugged the jeans down and stared at them with disgust.

"I paid a hundred bucks for those bad boys," I muttered as I tossed them into the trash next to his desk.

My eyes caught on something silver, and I bent down and picked up the foil packet.

"Why do you have condoms in your trash?" I questioned, holding up the offensive object.

He looked at it and grinned. "It was in the bowl you knocked over with the pencil holder. My assistant coach thinks it's hilarious to put a bowl of them on my desk so that the players will have easy access to them if they need to."

As he spoke, he bent over and picked up a handful of them from somewhere beyond the desk where the rest must've fallen, and I looked at them with wide eyes.

"And the boys have no problem coming in here and taking them?" I questioned.

"Nope," he said. "And I have no problem with them taking them. If they need them, I'd rather they come get them than to do anything stupid. Though, that day I first saw you and gave you a bloody nose at Target? I was buying my nephew them because I caught him in a car with his current flavor of the month steaming it up."

I looked away, faced once again with how embarrassing that encounter had been.

"Ready," I said softly, slipping back into my shoes.

They looked ridiculous with the too large sweats, but it's not like I had a choice in the matter at this point.

"Let's go grab the tea," he ordered.

Five minutes later, Ezra was loaded down with four gallons of sweet tea, and I had two, as we walked back into the staff meeting.

Everyone and their brother looked up.

"Sorry it took so long," Ezra drawled with four gallons of sweet tea in his beautiful hands. "Ms. Crusie caught her pants on the corner of the crappy staff kitchen counter and ripped them. I had to go find her a pair of my spare workout sweats."

A few of the teachers snickered, and Coach Casper narrowed her eyes at me.

I flushed and looked away, placing the gallons of tea on the counter next to the cups that someone else had provided, and hurried to the seat I'd been previously occupying.

Nobody was surprised in the least that I'd ripped my pants.

I knew why.

I was *that* much of a klutz.

Nobody was surprised by the fact that I'd done something embarrassing, not even the new teachers.

Ezra took a seat next to me and crossed his legs extending them out in front of him, while also crossing his arms over his chest.

The stance screamed comfort, and I wanted to punch him in the nuts for his casualness.

He was acting like he hadn't just rocked my world outside the auditorium where my peers and freakin' boss were waiting for us to arrive.

But I was happy, too.

Why?

Because he didn't sit by Coach Casper, and I knew she could tell that Ezra and I were something.

Hell, the way he leaned toward me said more than words alone.

CHAPTER 13

Let's eat Grandma. Let's eat, Grandma.

-Ezra explaining why punctuation is important

Ezra

Not only was her house covered in toilet paper, but the side yard trees were, too.

Hell, it even extended into the back.

And when I looked over her fence for a quick peek, I cursed.

She had trees down...*everywhere.*

And one of those trees had a branch that had busted in her back porch and patio roof.

My eyes scanned the rest of the yard surveying all of the damage.

None of which she could clean up on her own.

I growled low under my breath and then sighed as I walked up to the front porch.

I didn't bother knocking, though.

Instead, I dropped my phone and keys on the first step, downed half of my water, and then set it directly next to them.

Then I went to work gathering toilet paper, going as far as to climb up into the tree to get most of it.

I was shirtless in blue jeans and my work boots when Raleigh finally came outside at ten that morning. By that point, I'd been working non-stop for over two hours, and I was definitely ready for a drink.

"Hey," she said huskily. "You want something to eat or drink?"

Was it bad to say that I wanted her to eat?

"You make any coffee yet?" I asked, coming up to stand with a hand at both hips.

She nodded.

"That and a cup of ice water," I said. "And I need some trash bags, too. The trash cans are full, and we're going to have to start stuffing these sticks into something else."

She turned and hurried back inside, and I swallowed as I got a load of her shorts.

They were so short that she might as well be wearing only underwear.

And they were so tight that I knew for a fact that she likely didn't have anything on underneath of them.

"Hey, Coach!"

I turned and saw one of my first period students, Mark Simpleton, standing there with his dog on a leash.

I raised a hand. "Hey, Mark. How are you?"

He grinned. "A lot better than you, it looks like."

He took a look around the yard. "Mackie struck again."

"What?" I asked, heart starting to thunder in my chest.

"Uhhh," he paused. "You…Mackie…shit."

I crossed my arms over my chest and gave him my best teacher stare.

"Talk," I ordered.

Mark's shoulders drooped. "Everyone knows Mackie does this to people that piss him off."

My brows lifted. "I didn't."

"It's all over the school. It's not a secret. Just listen."

With that, he rushed away, the poor little dog with his too-short legs barely keeping up.

I felt anger stir in my belly at hearing that and wished I wasn't the 'cool' teacher. What Mark just said wouldn't have slipped out if it'd been Raleigh he'd been talking to. It was hard because I had to be careful of what I shared since the students treated me as one of them, which served my purposes most of the time.

However, now I needed to listen to word around the student body when it came to Mackie, and I didn't want to throw any of the students under the bus when I had to eventually confront the little fucker.

It'd been a long time coming but something needed to be done about that kid.

It didn't matter how good of a player he was. The little shit needed to learn that his behavior wasn't acceptable.

"Ezra?"

I turned to see Raleigh standing there, a cup of coffee in one hand, and a glass of water with two trash bags stuffed in the other.

I stalked toward her, my need for her starting to curl in my gut.

This woman was too good for words.

How had I never noticed her before this year?

I felt like an utter fool.

Reaching her, I took the coffee, and then leaned forward and took her mouth.

"Whew!" I heard exclaimed from behind us.

I broke the kiss and turned only my head to glare at the person over my shoulder. Another student—this one a girl.

I rolled my eyes. "Good morning, Ms. Chance."

Layla Chance waved her hands, her best friend Mindy Kreed next to her. "Hello, Ms. Crusie. Coach McDuff!"

I turned back around and looked down at Raleigh.

"What the hell? I've already seen three students this morning," I muttered, looking down at her.

Raleigh's cheeks were flushed with pleasure. "This is a popular walking area since we're so close to the trail, plus it's a family neighborhood. I think half the student population lives in this neighborhood with their parents. You'll see a lot more before the morning is over."

She was not lying.

I saw nearly the entire freakin' school, and I had a teeny-weeny inkling that the only reason I saw as many as I did was because I was shirtless working on Raleigh's lawn.

The only reason I saw the females, anyway. The male student population was around because the student female population was.

Grinning, I got back to work. At least until the cry of Mother Nature came calling.

I knocked on Raleigh's door where she'd disappeared about an hour ago and waited for her to appear. She did about a minute later, covered head to toe in flour and what looked like chocolate.

I grinned as she pushed open her screen door with one elbow.

"Uhh," I teased. "You look a little rough."

She blew some of her hair out of her eyes, but it fell right back into place.

She sighed.

I helped her out by tucking it behind her ear.

"I gotta use the bathroom, then I'll finish," I said.

"I'll change so I can help," she murmured softly, waving her hand at her clothes in explanation.

I grinned at her attire.

She had on another pair of tight jeans, these even tighter than the ones that she had on yesterday. She was also wearing a pair of worn-in cowboy boots that were definitely not something that you worked in. Not with those pointy-assed toes and sparkly pink glitter decorative tassels.

"Don't change on my account," I said. "But the toilet paper is almost out, I just have the stuff at the top to get. Then we can start on the back…if you have time and something to feed me with."

She grinned. "I just made fried chicken and mashed potatoes, but they have to cook in the oven for a few minutes. That's my mama's secret to the ultimate crispiness on the breading. Once that's done, we can eat, and then I'll help you."

I dabbed at a bit of chocolate on her cheek and showed it to her on one outstretched finger.

"And this?" I teased.

She smiled, her eyes flicking up to mine. "Dessert."

I felt things in my belly clench.

"What if what I want for dessert is you?" I teased.

I felt all of her attention focus on me.

"I'd say yes, absolutely a hundred percent yes, but you were the one who told me you had something to do today," she pointed out.

I did, indeed, have something to do later today. I had to go eat with my parents, and I fully planned on bringing her along.

She just didn't know it yet.

I hadn't wanted to tell her because I knew she'd likely freak out and try to overanalyze everything, so I figured springing it on her was in my best interest.

"Bathroom…then I'll climb that tree and take care of the last little bit." I bopped her on the nose with one finger. "And I want to take you with me later if that's okay. It's nothing fancy or anything. In fact, what you're wearing right now is perfect. Well, minus the chocolate streaks and flour dusting."

She looked down at her boots and blushed. "I liked them," she tried to explain them away.

I grinned. "I like them, too, darlin'."

With that, I walked down her hallway to the bathroom and shut the door.

I heard the screen door bang closed, signaling she'd gone outside and felt more than comfortable to take my time.

Only, I likely shouldn't have.

Why?

Because the woman that I freakin' loved was a goddamn lunatic, that's why.

Why was she a lunatic?

Well, when I came outside, it was to find her boots off in the middle of the yard, and a pair of mismatched socks not far away.

The second thing that I saw was Raleigh, about halfway up the tree, trying to reach some toilet paper with one of those grabber thing-a-ma-jigs that lets handicapped—and lazy—people pick stuff up off the floor without bending over.

She was stretched out on a limb precariously, and not only was her arm extended as far as she could get it to go, but she was also holding the grabber out in front of her, too. She was inches away from grabbing the long piece of toilet paper when my brain finally caught up with what she was doing, and I felt my heart jump out of my chest.

"Are you out of your freakin' mind?" I bellowed.

Raleigh shrieked…and that's how she fell out of the tree and broke her arm.

***

Raleigh glared at me. "Don't you even think about it."

I opened her door and stepped back.

"I can't believe you're making me come here," she grumbled.

I grinned. "We didn't get to eat your lunch, and I'm starving, Raleigh. Plus, my parents asked me to stop by to pick something up," I lied.

She gave me a calculating look, then waved her casted hand in my direction.

"I'm also mad at you," she grumbled. "This is all your fault."

My brows rose as I slammed the truck door closed just a little bit harder than I should have.

"What are you talking about?" I accused.

I put one hand on her back and guided her up the front walk of my parents' house, hearing the commotion of little feet running inside.

Moira's high-pitched 'Daddy, higher' had me grinning despite the accusations coming from Raleigh's mouth.

"Then, let me get this straight," I said after she finished. "You're blaming me for you falling out of the tree because I yelled?"

She nodded.

"And why the hell were you up there in the first place?" I questioned, seemingly for the eighth time. "I told you I was going to go up there."

She shrugged. "I didn't want you to get hurt."

That'd been her answer seven out of eight. The first time I'd asked, when she was getting her arm straightened out, was to say 'go fuck yourself.'

I wasn't holding that answer against her.

My brows rose. "And you think that I wanted *you* to get hurt?"

She shrugged nonchalantly. "It is my house that this happened to. If one of us was going to get hurt, it should be me."

"I've been climbing trees since I was old enough to wear shoes," I told her as I opened the screen door and gestured her inside. "Trust me when I say, there was no danger from me falling out. Can you say the same about yourself?"

"Aunt Raleigh!" Moira screeched. "You have a cast! Can I sign it?"

Raleigh's smile was not forced when she greeted my niece. "Of course. Do you have a Sharpie marker?"

Moira didn't ask why or how the cast came to be, only if she could sign it.

That girl.

"What happened?" my sister asked, sounding concerned.

"Aunt Raleigh fell out of a tree," Colton said, sounding bored. "I saw it happen. I was across the street at Cristopher's house. Uncle Ezra yelled at her and startled her. Then she fell out."

Raleigh shot me a triumphant smile as if to say, 'See?'

"I didn't think she'd fall out of the tree when I yelled at her, or I never would've done it!" I shot a quelling look over at my nephew.

"Oh, we're more than aware of that," Johnson said. "And, also, everyone at the school knows y'all are banging now, too. We saw that kiss. We saw the look in both of your eyes. There's no lying about the fact that y'all are together."

Raleigh gasped, but I only shrugged.

"I wasn't trying to hide anything," I admitted. "There's not a no-fraternization policy, and I haven't been quiet about my feelings for her. It's not my fault that y'all are just exceptionally unobservant."

"We're not that unobservant," Johnson explained. "Mackie was the one to call it that y'all were together. He said y'all were f-u-c-k-i-n-g," Johnson spelled it out so Moira, who'd arrived with her Sharpie, couldn't understand the bad word. "The day that you made us apologize to her. Even though, technically, I wasn't the one in the wrong."

I blinked. "Mackie said that?"

Johnson shrugged, his eyes going away from his Xbox for a few short, precious seconds, before returning to the screen. "Yep. He was also adamant that he was going to get you back. I'm guessing he's started with Raleigh, knowing you like her. Toilet papering has begun—and that's his signature move. That's usually only the first step, though."

"What's his next step?" my sister asked.

Johnson cursed quietly under his breath when he died, and he leaned forward and dropped the controller onto the couch cushion beside his hips. "He's a douche. It only gets worse, but usually this is all reserved for kids. I've never seen him get mad at a teacher before. I don't know his next step. Last fall, when Talia Rimmel broke up with him, he TP-ed her house, and then ran his tractor into her car...with her in it."

I had a sick feeling inside my chest, and I didn't like it one single bit.

"Great," I muttered. "What a little prick."

"Yep," Johnson agreed and stood up. "I have a date. I'll check y'all losers later."

With that, he walked out the door, and we all watched him go.

I looked over to Raleigh, who was busy holding very still for Moira, who was drawing Elsa and Olaf on her ice blue cast, chattering away about the next Frozen movie that was due to come out next year.

Raleigh's eyes lifted up and met mine, and she shrugged.

She'd heard the entire spiel as well, and I saw that she wasn't bothered by it.

At least that made one of us.

"Where's Dad?" I asked my sister, wanting to change the subject.

"Dad is in the, errrm, bedroom with Mom," my sister whispered.

"Granddad is giving it to Grandma," Moira chirped. "That's what he said through the door when I walked past their room to their office to get this Sharpie." She paused and looked up. "Whatever that's supposed to mean."

Every adult in the room, as well as Johnson who hadn't quite made it out the door, gagged.

"That's disgusting," Johnson groaned as he slammed the door behind him. "I'm not coming back!"

I wished I hadn't come at all.

***

Dinner, at first, was an awkward affair.

My parents, not realizing anyone was in their house, had gone about doing what they wanted to do—i.e., each other.

While we, my sister, her husband and my best friend, as well as Raleigh and I sat on the couch not speaking until they were done.

The kids had played quietly in the yard.

Which led us to now, all of us sitting at the table, eating in silence.

Of course, it had to be Raleigh that broke that silence.

"I once walked in on my parents doing it on the kitchen table," she murmured. "I wouldn't eat there for a year."

There was silence for a few long seconds, and then I started to crack up.

"Oh, God," my mother wheezed. "At least we keep it to our bedroom. But, just sayin', it'll teach y'all to knock or announce yourselves before you walk into our house."

"I texted," Cady said in outrage. "I mean, what more did you want me to do? Have one of those criers from the old days announce my presence before I arrive?"

My pop snorted. "How about we just change the subject, and we act like it never happened?" he suggested.

"But it did happen," Raleigh offered helpfully. "I don't mind, though. It's a natural thing. It wasn't like y'all were doing anything illegal."

I groaned and leaned my head against the back of my chair. "Is there a reason we're still talking about this? I don't feel like this is something that we should continue to talk about over my favorite dinner."

"It is his favorite dinner," my mom amended. "We can talk about this after dinner, during dessert if you're more comfortable."

"How about never?" Cady suggested.

"You do know, right, that your father and I had sex, which then turned into conceiving you," my mother teased, enjoying the fact that she could embarrass her adult children, just like she enjoyed it when we were younger. "There's this thing called conception, it starts by…"

"La-la-la-la-la," Cady yelled loudly. "I'm not listening."

"What's sex, Grandma?" Moira asked suddenly, appearing at our sides with a Gatorade and handing it to her father, who twisted it open without a second's thought. "I want to have sex!"

That was when the entire table exploded, while Raleigh watched on in fascination.

CHAPTER 14

333. I'm only half evil.

-Text from Raleigh to Camryn

Raleigh

"Ms. Crusie?" the office called over the speaker in my classroom. "Do you have a moment to come into my office and speak with me?"

I looked up in horror at the speaker and then looked at the students that were huddling in my classroom to escape the rain outside where they would normally be having their lunch period.

"Yes, ma'am," I said to the old office lady, Mrs. Johns. "I'll be there in ten minutes."

It just so happened that not only was I forced to take the senior sex-ed class, I was also forced to take the classroom that was as far away from civilization, as well as the office, as it could be.

Not that I was complaining.

I loved the classroom…mostly.

But, every once in a while, a few doubts and fears would creep in, and I'd be left thinking that nobody would hear us—or me—if we screamed.

"Awww, man!" Johnson whined. "I'm only half done with my math homework for Uncle Ezra's class."

I stood up and gathered my keys. "I'll allow y'all to stay in here on two conditions."

Morgan, who'd been helping Johnson, looked up. "And what's that?"

"Y'all don't trash my crap, and y'all don't try to pry open the desk drawers to get a peek at your test."

It was Mackie's snort of derision that almost had me reaching into the desk and withdrawing the tests. Morgan and Johnson were okay. Mackie? Not so much.

Luckily, and unluckily as I saw it, the classroom we were in was also the same classroom that I taught sex-ed in, meaning that the students had gathered there to study during lunch. I didn't mind. I was beginning to really enjoy that particular group of kids, sans a few bad apples.

I also couldn't wait to hand over the tests.

I'd changed them up a little from the norm, and I had a feeling that today's test wouldn't be as easy as the last two had been.

Apparently, someone was handing out the answers, and not one single person had made below a ninety the entire semester.

Though this was an easy class, it wasn't the type of class that would have every single student passing every single test with flying colors.

Life just didn't work like that.

I'd expected at least one B, because I hadn't made the test easy, but they were all doing well.

Sure, some of them I'd expect to actually read the material and study, like Johnson and Morgan.

However, Mackie making a ninety-nine when he refused to do any of his homework, or even open a book, left something inside of me suspicious of his actions.

"Yes, ma'am," Johnson drawled. "We'll be good. Pinky promise."

He held up his pinky, and jokingly I walked over to him and took the pinky with mine.

Afterward, I walked out of the class and toward the office, feeling dread replace my calm before I'd even made it halfway.

It didn't help that I saw Ezra coming out of the principal's office just as I was arriving.

It also scared me when he wouldn't look at me as he passed.

By the time I was sitting in front of Mrs. Sherpa's desk, I was a nervous wreck.

"We had a parent log a complaint about you," Mrs. Sherpa said, not beating around the bush.

My brows rose.

"Okay," I paused. "What about?"

I was thinking it was one of my calculus student's parents who were unhappy with how I was grading their child. I couldn't be farther from the truth.

"We would like you to know that the complaint will be investigated, but we don't foresee anything following the investigation. But, by law, we have to investigate," she explained.

I was flabbergasted.

"What was the complaint?" I repeated.

She wiggled in her seat. "The parent said that you made a comment to a male student, and when the male student told their parents what you said, they felt that it was a sexual advance."

My mouth fell open.

"What?"

"It happened in your sex-ed class," she explained. "And apparently, you asked the student a question about something in the textbook, and you made a sexual innuendo as you did."

My mind raced.

I had no idea who she was talking about, or what I might've said.

"I teach straight out of the book," I explained, trying to relay how I taught. "Honestly, I follow the chapters, and give tests straight out of the books exactly like Coach McDuff did previously. Nothing that I've done can or will ever be misconstrued as a sexual advance toward any student. Honestly, those students scare the absolute bejesus out of me, and you very well know it."

She nodded in understanding. "I know. Which is why I don't think the investigation will go anywhere. For the time being, though, Coach McDuff will be taking over the class until the investigation is taken care of."

That explained Ezra's panicked look as he exited the office and saw me standing there.

He knew.

Oh, God. I felt like a fool.

And I felt sick to my stomach.

I'd never once said a word to my students that could ever be misconstrued as anything other than appropriate.

I was *not* that kind of teacher that played around with her students—I literally couldn't handle that.

And everyone knew it.

Why hadn't Ezra said something?

Did he believe her?

"What about my regular classes?" I asked carefully.

"Those you can continue since the student that complained wasn't attending those." She paused. "I don't want you to think that we don't believe you, because we do."

I waited.

"But with the student's parents being who they are, the school board will overrule me if I don't follow through on this to the letter." She gave me a sympathetic look. "This happens, so don't fret. But, be careful of what you say, and if anything happens that you think I should know about, don't hesitate to share it with me, okay?"

I mentally reviewed things that I thought she might want to know about and other than Ezra and I having a relationship outside of school, I was coming up empty.

"Okay," I sighed and stood up.

With my next period now suddenly free, I wasn't sure what to do with myself.

All of my work that I'd brought was back in my classroom where I was sure Ezra was on his way to, but I wasn't sure what I should do.

"Can I go back and get my stuff?" I asked. "Or should I wait until after school?"

She shooed me away with her hand. "Go back and get it."

I did, leaving the principal's office behind.

I was so caught up in my own thoughts that I wasn't prepared for the hand that came around my arm to jerk me to a stop.

The fingers bit into the fat of my armpit, and I cried out in pain.

My eyes jerked up, and I found myself face to face with Mackie.

I glowered, jerking my arm away, and put distance between us.

All the while, my heart pounded.

Before I could ask him what had happened, or anything about why he'd squeezed so hard, Ezra rounded the corner, a scowl on his face.

When he saw Mackie standing so close to me, his scowl darkened.

"Back up, Mackie," Ezra barked.

"Sorry, Coach." Mackie backed away with his hands in the air. "I didn't want her to fall. Floor's wet."

I looked down, and sure enough, the floor was wet.

But I'd been in no danger of falling.

I had on fairly slip-resistant shoes, but Mackie's words did ring true when he explained his actions.

My arm still throbbed where he'd gripped me, but I couldn't very well contradict the kid.

I was prone to busting my ass—and had actually done that quite a few times.

Many of which had been in this very hallway.

Needless to say, I was not the most graceful of teachers.

"Thanks," I murmured, trying not to rub my arm and tip Ezra off. "I didn't know it was wet."

Mackie's eyes didn't show a hint of anything.

No anger. No pity. No derision. No happiness. No nothing.

It was weird, really.

But before I could think to say anything else, Morgan rounded the corner, a look of worry on his face.

"Uh, Coach?" Morgan paused. "Ms. Crusie? Someone broke into your desk. All your stuff is spread out all over the classroom. Johnson and Mackie helped me to the bathroom, and we weren't in there for five minutes tops."

Forgetting the wet floor, I took off in the direction of the senior hallway, as well as my classroom that wasn't my classroom any longer.

I came to a halt in the doorway with Ezra standing right behind me.

His growl made my chest vibrate.

Heart in my throat, I walked into the room and scowled at all the papers—the tests—and my things that were scattered everywhere. My gradebook was also ripped to shreds, as well as any receipt that was in my purse.

Hell, even my tampons had been opened and thrown all over the floor.

The money from my wallet was splayed across the desk, and all of my spare change was on the floor surrounding where my purse had been hastily dumped.

The only thing that wasn't a mess was the answer sheet, which was clearly displayed in front of the entire room full of students—which were early for once, likely due to the commotion.

"Shit," Ezra pushed past me to gather my things.

I picked up my phone and keys, followed shortly by my money.

Ezra got the extras, like my toothpaste and mini-toothbrush.

I picked up the tests last and threw them in the trash.

It didn't matter now what I would've used. I was no longer the teacher for this course, and since it was nearing the end of school anyway, it didn't really matter any longer.

Once my things were cleaned up, I smiled at the students—at least the ones that weren't looking at me with blank faces—i.e., Mackie.

I headed to the door without another word, and Johnson was the one to stop me.

"Where are you going?" he asked.

I turned to survey the group. "Ezra—Coach McDuff—has decided to take the class back over. Now that he's found time again."

See, the thing about teenagers, they knew damn well when someone was lying—like I was doing right then.

Yet, none of them called me on it.

Without another word, I walked out of the room and told myself I wouldn't cry.

I managed not to until I got to the staff bathroom and shut the door.

Then I cried for as long as I could without it being more than obvious that something was wrong.

I came out to find Camryn stuffing a donut into her face.

She was mid-chew when she got a load of my puffy eyes.

"What's wrong?" she asked in alarm.

I looked down at my hands. "I got a student/parent complaint. They said I made a sexual advance toward a student, and that I will not be teaching that class any longer."

Her mouth fell open. "They what?"

I nodded. "Yep."

"You wouldn't do that!" she cried out. "Out of any teacher in this school, I'd expect it from all of us before you!"

I would, too.

Yet, there was nothing I could do about it.

"What are you going to do?" she questioned.

I walked over and took the rest of her donut. She gave it up without a fight.

"I'm going to teach my other classes and enjoy my new free period I guess," I muttered, stuffing the entire bite into my mouth without another word.

Lani Lynn Vale

CHAPTER 15

Hold on. Let me overthink this.

-Text from Raleigh to Ezra

Raleigh

Getting in trouble did not sit well with me.

Hence the reason I was sitting in a bar, drunk off my hiney, with Camryn at my side just as drunk.

I couldn't tell you why this bar in particular.

Honestly, neither Camryn nor I were much into drinking, so it didn't take much to garner our attention.

And when we read 'real life rodeo bull inside,' we'd decided that this particular bar, 'Ride Em Joe's,' was the one we'd be drinking at that night.

We were a town over in case things—or we—got out of hand, and neither one of us were feeling any pain.

Well, Camryn hadn't been feeling much pain to begin with since she wasn't the one in trouble.

Me, on the other hand? Well, I was feeling pain, but I was able to forget about it while I drank nasty beer after nasty beer.

I'd never been a fan of beer before, but after the fourth watered-down cup, I didn't particularly care anymore.

It all tasted the same, and Camryn was getting funnier and funnier by the second.

"Do you think that Ezra will have boy children or girl children?" Camryn questioned.

I swiveled my head to stare at her where she was perched on the barstool next to me.

"I would think that it's possible to have both genders," I paused. "Why are you asking me that?"

Camryn shrugged. "Because I can. Do you think your brother will get married one day?"

Croft, the man that my best friend had a crush on since we were in college together. All it'd taken was one single time of Camryn coming home with me over the holidays for the crush to become concrete.

Seemed we were both doomed to only fall for one man, and one man only.

And like Ezra, Croft didn't even know that Camryn was alive.

Logically, he of course knew that she was a person, and my best friend. But he didn't see her as anything but that. It didn't matter what Camryn dressed like, or how much she put herself out there. Croft was so freakin' focused on whatever the hell Croft focused on that he didn't even see her.

Just like Ezra didn't see me—not until he'd knocked me down and bloodied my nose, anyway.

"Oh, boy."

I looked over to Camryn, blinking to try to get the haze out of my vision.

Unfortunately, it seemed like it was there to stay, because I couldn't make it go away.

But, since I was drunk, I also didn't care.

"I don't know," I told her honestly. "My brother is a pain in the ass...we should just call him."

Camryn giggled. "Your brother doesn't answer your phone calls...what makes you think he'll answer this one?"

I knew that.

Croft only responded to text...hours after they were sent to him.

But, since I had nothing else to lose tonight, and I was feeling quite wild, I dialed his number, put him on speaker phone, and then waited for him not to answer.

I'd had grand plans to leave him a long, drawn-out voicemail.

However, to my surprise, as well as Camryn's, he answered.

"'Lo?"

I gasped. "You answered!"

There was a long pause where I could practically envision Croft contemplating hanging up on me, but since he'd answered, I knew as well as he did that he was stuck talking to me.

"I didn't mean to," he admitted. "I was going to send the call to voicemail and reply with a text, but my fat fingers pressed the wrong button...where are you? It's loud."

I looked around the bar.

For a Thursday night, it was quite restrained. In fact, I wouldn't even call it very loud.

I mean, I could hear him. That was an indication right there as to how loud it wasn't.

"I'm at a bar." I licked my lips. "Croft, do you think you'll ever get married?"

There was a long pause again, and then he said, "No. Not right now, anyway. Why are you asking?"

"Camryn wanted to know…ouch!" I cried out as Camryn's palm met the flesh of my thigh. "What was that for, Camryn? Seriously, I swear to God. If you hit me again, I'm going to punch you in the nipple."

Camryn flicked me on the arm, and I did exactly what I said I was going to do—punch her in the nipple.

"Owwww!" Camryn whined. "Holy hell. Was that really necessary?"

"Girls," Croft growled. "If there was no reason for your call, I'm going to have to let you go. I'm out on a date."

Camryn and I both gasped. "You're out on a date?" I screeched.

"Yes," Croft said tiredly. "I am. Is that okay?"

"No," I immediately disagreed. "You canceled dinner plans to go out on a date with someone? Do you know what happened to me today? I was fired!"

"You were *what*?" Croft barked.

"She's lying," Camryn soothed Croft's pique of temper. "She wasn't fired from all of her classes. Just the one. But only because she was accused of sexual favors."

There was a third long pause, and then Croft groaned in frustration. "Don't drive, you two. I'll be there in a little bit."

"You don't even know where 'there' is," I pointed out. "And I'm not talking to you right now, you blew me off. I just can't deal with your rude self."

Croft moaned.

"I'm sorry," Croft lied through his big, fat, buck teeth.

Camryn snorted.

I flat out laughed, which turned into a coughing fit because I was also trying to take a sip of my drink.

"Does your coach know where you are?" Croft asked silkily.

"No," I said. "Because the butthead was the one to take over my class. I suffered through that class this year! Can you believe it? I was a freakin' virgin when I started that class. I'm sure half of those students knew more than I did about freakin' sex, yet I taught it because I was told to. And I started to overcome my fears! Then what do I have to show for it? They're all going to remember stupid Ezra now, and not me."

"Stupid Ezra?" Croft laughed. "I dare you to say that to his face."

I just very well might.

"Bye, brother," I said, then threw the phone down on the table.

I vaguely remembered that there was something else I probably should've done, but then the blinking light over the bull started to flash, indicating that the bull was free, momentarily distracting me.

Both Camryn and I watched in fascination as some buxom blonde climbed up, her dress hiking up to her hips and exposing her nearly see-through lace panties.

Then the bull started to move and twist, slowly at first, followed shortly by jerkier up and down movements.

Each twist had her breasts jiggling precariously in the small, spaghetti-strapped black dress until suddenly the bull jolted forward and knocked her ass over tea kettle onto the ground.

She sat up laughing her ass off, and that was when Camryn turned to me.

"We have to do that," she ordered.

I bit my lip, looking warily at the bull, and shook my head. "I dunno…"

I looked down at my cast, then back up at her.

"Come on," she pleaded.

It took me another entire drink to agree, and only then did I say yes if she went first.

Which was what she did moments later.

Camryn hurried to the bull, her hand on the banister that led to the lower stage, allowing everyone in the establishment to see what was happening down below.

And then she stood beside the bull and thought about the best way to get up onto it.

"Run and jump!" I hollered.

Camryn flipped me off with a small grin on her face.

I grinned back, then called out a 'woo hoo!' to her as she started to mount it.

Camryn had just climbed up on the bull around the time that Croft walked in the door with his date, momentarily distracting me from Camryn's start.

I gasped and started down the stairs, wanting to get a better look at Camryn's face when she realized that my brother had seen her ride.

By the time she was bucked off moments later, I was standing beside where she was sprawled indelicately on the mat and we were both laughing.

I climbed onto the mat and wrapped my arms around her. "Oh, God! That was great!"

Camryn held onto my head and pulled me to her side, shaking with her laughter. "That was fun, you should go!"

I stood up, wobbled, and then reached for the bull to steady myself.

My gaze was caught by a commotion at the stairs, and that was when I saw Coach Butthead heading down toward me.

"That sounds like the best thing I've ever heard!" I declared.

Then, before my brother or Coach Grumpy Pants could stop me, I climbed on the bull and pointed at the man controlling it. "Hit it!"

The bull controller 'hit it' and then I was hanging on for dear life while also trying not to laugh my ass off in the process.

I even got one second longer before I, too, went flying just as easily as Camryn had moments before.

I hit the mat hard and awkwardly.

My casted arm hit the metal underneath the bull that controlled its movements, and I cried out as pain radiated up my elbow and into my heart.

"Owwww," I whined, my drunkenness clearing the tiniest of bits. "That hurt!"

Then I rolled over to see a pair of black Under Armour wind pants with our school mascot on them standing next to my face.

I rolled over onto my back and looked up the long, lean body of Coach McDuff, and wondered if this was heaven.

Surely it had to be.

But then I got to his face and saw he was scowling at me.

It must be hell.

"Am I in hell?" I asked the coach that was glaring at me.

"No, but you might wish you were after I'm through with you," he growled irately.

Oh, Coach McDuff was *pissed*.

He reached down for my good arm, and I slapped him away. "Don't touch me, Coach Cheater McCheaterson."

Ezra ignored me and hauled me up to standing beside him, causing my world to tilt on its axis for a few long seconds.

"Whoa," I chortled. "That was fun!"

"Are you drunk?" he asked, sounding just as miffed as he had been when I was lying down.

"I don't know," I admitted. "Until today, I've never drunk a single alcoholic beverage before! What does drunk look like?"

"You," my brother grunted as he stared at me. "I can almost see your boobs."

I looked down at said boobs. "I have a t-shirt on."

"You have a freakin' tank top on, and you're not wearing a bra," he challenged.

I frowned. "I am, too." I then pulled my bra strap out of my tank top to show the dumbass. "See?"

"Do something with her, she's embarrassing me," my brother ordered the man holding onto me.

I started to push away. "No! I have things to do!"

"No, you don't," Ezra disagreed. "In fact, you have to work tomorrow, so it's probably best that you stop drinking now. With any luck, I can get some coffee and water in you and make you halfway presentable for tomorrow. You got Camryn?"

"I'm not going to work tomorrow," I declared. "I quit!"

"You're not quitting, hoe!" Camryn yelled. "If you quit, then who will I talk about all the great asses of the school to?"

"That's gross," the woman, Croft's date, said. "Those are children."

Camryn looked over at the woman, who likely shouldn't be privy to this conversation. "I was talking about Coach McDuff," she hitched a thumb in Ezra's direction. "And the assistant coach. And the girls' softball coach, as well as one of the science teachers—he's new this year, and yowza, does he have one fine ass. It was a tossup between him and Coach McDuff this year, to be honest. Not children, you freakin' loser."

"What about Officer Flint?" I teased her.

Camryn's mouth tightened, and her eyes narrowed. Her finger went straight as a board as she pointed it at me.

"Do not speak about that man in my presence again," she ordered. "That man is a lying, despicable, no good, rotten, disgusting, arrogant, asshole, big, fat…"

Croft slapped his hand over Camryn's mouth, but something in his eyes told me he was trying not to laugh.

Ezra scooped me up then, and in his haste to toss me over his shoulder, I knocked the beer that had miraculously appeared in Camryn's hand onto the ground, half of the beer slinking down inside my cast as I did.

"Shit!" I hissed. "That's cold!"

It wasn't until we were outside, and I was on my feet next to Ezra's truck, that he saw my problem.

"We'll go get it changed," he said. "Then we're going home."

He was true to his word, taking me to the twenty-four-hour emergency clinic to get my cast changed before taking us to my home.

"Keys?" he asked.

I shook my head. "I don't have any. I rode with Camryn."

He grunted, his eyes never leaving mine. "So how are you going to get into the house?"

I turned to the door and twisted the knob. "I didn't bother locking it."

He muttered something else behind me that sounded like 'stupid,' but I couldn't be sure.

"What?"

CHAPTER 16

Please do not pet the peeves.

-T-shirt

Ezra

I'd lost every bit of patience I had left, and it was all because of the woman looking at me with such fucking innocence in her eyes.

She had no clue what she did to me.

She also had no clue that her tears nearly brought me to my knees.

I hated walking out of the principal's office today. I hated it even more to see her tears rolling down her cheeks after she realized that I'd be taking over.

It took me about two hours to find out why she'd been removed from the class, and once that had happened, I'd lost nearly all of my patience.

I'd talked to Mrs. Sherpa, letting her know that Raleigh and I were in a relationship. I'd also let her know in no uncertain terms that out of anyone in the school, Raleigh was the least likely teacher to do anything like that ever.

She agreed with me, and also told me to keep my relationship out of the school as best that I could—which we would.

But I was done hiding what I felt for the woman currently drunk off her ass standing in front of me.

I was also tired as hell of hiding the fact that I cared for her a whole lot more than I ever thought I'd care about a woman.

"Despite what you think, it's not safe to keep your doors unlocked," I growled, trying valiantly to control my temper.

She snickered. "Ezra Wezra, this is Gun Barrel. We have a population of twenty thousand. Plus, I have that alarm sticker on my window."

I grunted. "You have an alarm sticker on your window…and you think that's helpful?"

She shrugged and started to strip, her shirt first, followed shortly by her bra.

The bra got caught up on her new cast, and she hastily pulled on it to get it unstuck.

The moment it came free of the cast, it slung across the empty room, and my eyes followed it.

Something caught my eye, and I frowned.

"What's that?" I pointed.

Raleigh snickered. "Camryn found that at a garage sale today on the way over to my house. Isn't it cute?"

It was something.

"Is it real?" I asked as my hand hovered over the stuffed cat.

The very real looking stuffed cat.

"No," she answered, starting on her jeans. "It's fake. Touch it."

"I'd rather touch something else," I murmured, liking the view in her direction a lot better.

She finally got to her underwear and shoved those down, too, leaving her in nothing but her short little ankle socks that I hadn't seen she had on inside her ankle boots.

Once those were off, she stared at me expectantly.

I was too preoccupied with her breasts to notice that she was expecting something from me.

"Well, let's go!" she declared.

I frowned. "Let's go?"

"Yes," she said, bending over the couch. "Do me!"

I chuckled.

"What if I didn't want to 'do' you?" I rumbled, coming up behind her.

She closed her eyes and smiled sweetly. "Then I guess I could go to sleep right here."

I chuckled, having no doubt in my mind that she might very well do it if I left her there for too long.

"Maybe sleep is the best thing you could have right now," I contemplated.

She snickered, her eyes opening to slits. "I've heard that drunk sex is better than sex."

I bit my lip to hold the laughter in. "Drunk sex, I think, is categorized under actual 'sex.'"

Her pursed lips told me she was actually contemplating what I said with all the seriousness that she could muster at that moment in time.

She pushed up on her elbows and glared at me. "Ezra McDuff...you have one job right now."

My brow rose. "Yeah?"

"Yeah," she confirmed. "And if you don't get to it, you lose boyfriend points. You've already lost some after the day I had…so I'd suggest you doing extra credit to make up for it."

The idea of doing anything 'extra credit' with her really turned me on. Like, *really* turned me on.

I bit my lip as ideas started to roll through my head rapid fire, one after the other.

"Extra credit?" I teased, finally pressing my hand against the soft skin of her ass and rubbing down the length of her thigh lightly. "What kind of extra credit?"

She spread her thighs.

"The kind where I get to feel that beard between my legs." She pointed down.

I felt adrenaline start to burn through my veins and my dick that'd been hard since I saw her the first time tonight stiffened further.

But I didn't want her where she was at.

I wanted her on her back on the bed, her hands free to pull and tug on my hair when my mouth was doing things between her thighs.

Without waiting for permission, I walked up behind her and picked her up around the waist.

She squealed in surprise, drunkenly clutching for the furniture that was no longer near her and giggled as I carried her into the bedroom.

The moment I was close enough to the bed, I tossed her and grinned when she continued to laugh her ass off.

She bounced twice before she finally sat still, her hair covering half of her face and her hands high above her head.

She blew the hair on her face, but all it did was go straight up and fall even more distractedly over her eyes and nose.

She tried it again, and then inhaled it, coughing moments later.

I put one knee into the bed and reached forward, wiping her hair away from her face.

If she hadn't been so drunk, I was sure that she'd be able to accomplish that feat on her own, yet I was happy to do it for her.

Honestly, I'd be happy to do just about anything as long as it was for her.

I looked down into her beautiful eyes and studied them.

She was staring at me with a small smile on her face.

"I love you, Raleigh Crusie," I growled, knowing she wouldn't remember in the morning.

Moments later, I dropped a hard, fast kiss on her upturned lips and pulled back before her grabby hands could make purchase in my hair.

"Sorry, Ms. Crusie, but I have extra credit to start working on," I teased, crawling my way down her body.

She shifted her legs, but the way my knees were positioned on either side of her thighs, she couldn't move them far before she got to the barrier.

"Ezra," she hissed. "Move!"

I snickered, moving first one knee, and then the other.

The moment she was free, she widened her legs and then pointed at her clit with one finger. "Right there, Coach McDuff."

I licked my lips, then dropped down onto my elbows, pressing my erection into the bed.

"Here?" I asked, kissing the inside of one thigh.

She shook her head, her eyes clearing up by the second. "No, here?"

She touched her clit again, and we both hissed.

"Here?" I moved closer, kissing the crease of her thigh.

"No," she wailed, her hand going to my hair. "Do you need me to guide you?"

I grinned against the skin of her thigh and nodded my head. "Maybe, Ms. Crusie."

She yanked on my hair, and I obediently looked up at her. "Will you follow the directions? Most don't."

I nodded. "Oh, yeah. I'm good at following directions."

That was a lie. I was totally a fly by the seat of my pants guy, but I'd tell her just about anything when she was in this mood.

I liked it when she was feisty.

"Okay," she said. "But if you don't listen, you're going to need to do some serious ass kissing to get the points you're losing back."

"Oh, no," I teased. "We can't have that."

She narrowed her eyes and pulled on my hair. "Up."

I went up, nibbling my way to where she wanted me.

"Open your mouth," she ordered.

I did.

"Stick out your tongue," she continued.

I did that, too.

"Forward," she instructed.

I moved forward, feeling my saliva gather in my mouth in anticipation of tasting her.

Her pussy was so pretty, and I could see the clear fluid gathering at her entrance, giving away her excitement.

I wanted to taste her everywhere, but for now, I'd play her game, doing what she wanted.

Though, what she was wanting definitely wasn't displeasing.

In fact, I fuckin' loved every second of it.

Her hands in my hair, her taste in my mouth? Yeah, there wasn't anywhere else I would want to be but exactly where I was.

"Jesus," she gasped. "Push it inside."

I did, following her directions to the exact preciseness that I did all things in life.

There was no reason to half-ass anything.

I was never the type not to give it my all. That was why this thing with Raleigh was going so far, so fast.

I wanted her.

I'd always known what I wanted, and I trusted my gut.

My gut was telling me exactly what I should do—and that was take her and keep her.

Make her mine forever.

I wasn't at the point where I'd propose, but I knew that it wouldn't be long before I felt it was the right time.

"You're not paying attention." She yanked on the hair she had fisted in her hands. "Lick me!"

I liked this assertive, drunk Raleigh. I liked her a lot.

I made a mental note to get her drunk more often.

"Yes, ma'am," I teased.

Then I did what I wanted, and she forgot that she was supposed to give instructions.

It was when I'd brought her nearly to the brink of orgasm and stopped that she finally realized I wasn't doing as I was told. However, at that point, she was too far gone to care.

Before she had a chance to protest, I was yanking the rest of my clothes free and crawling up between her legs, thrusting inside. I gave her my full length without giving her a chance to adjust.

Which, in turn, had us both crying out. Her in surprise and pleasure, and me in such exquisite agony that I could barely find it in me to breathe.

Even though I'd had her regularly and had been masturbating on my own when she wasn't around to give it to me, I was on the brink before I'd even gotten three thrusts into that tight body of hers.

Everything was just so hot and wet that I couldn't function, let alone tell myself that it was too soon. That I hadn't been going long enough yet for either of our best interests.

But then she started to ripple around me, and I started to spurt inside of her in reaction.

I couldn't help it.

With Raleigh, she rendered me utterly useless when it came to making her mine.

"Fuck!" I snarled.

Or was it Raleigh?

I wasn't sure, to be honest.

But in the end, I wasn't sure that I really cared, because I was inside of her and everything in my life was fucking right.

For the first time in forever, I knew what I wanted out of life.

Her. Us. Me and her. Kids. Three. A house. Two cars. A white goddamn picket fence.

Everything all centered around her, though.

And as I looked into her eyes and saw the same feelings that I was currently feeling rising in my chest, I knew that we'd make this work.

I wasn't going to ask her to marry me today…but I knew it'd happen.

Soon.

"I love you, Raleigh."

She closed her eyes and smiled.

Then she turned her head on the pillow, with me still inside her, and started to snore.

I had no other recourse but to laugh.

Lani Lynn Vale

CHAPTER 17

I'm mom's favorite.

-Text from Raleigh to Croft

Raleigh

"Gotta go change and get to practice," Ezra growled against my mouth. "Be good."

I smiled into the semi-darkness, patting his muscular forearm, and falling right back to sleep.

At least, I would have had the words that I'd always wanted to hear not fallen from those perfect lips.

"Love you, Raleigh."

By the time I processed them, and realized that I needed to return the sentiment, he was already starting that loud truck of his up and backing out of my driveway.

I reached for my phone to type out a text but realized it wasn't by the bed.

Frowning, I got up, feeling something inside of my chest practically screaming in excitement, and started my search.

I found it all in the living room—my dress, shoes, and panties. My purse with my dead phone inside, and my Chapstick.

I made a girlish squeak of excitement as I snatched my phone up, leaving all the clothes where they were, and practically skipped to my room.

It wasn't until I'd jumped on the bed and dove for the charging cable, knocking my newly casted arm on the bedpost, that I told myself that I needed to calm down. If not for any other reason than to not re-break my already healing arm.

That would be something I'd do.

Plugging it in and leaving it on the bed to reboot, I rushed to the shower and turned it on.

My eyes went to the green bottle of Irish Spring body wash that Ezra had brought over the last time he'd spent the night and inhaled deeply as I relished the smell of him in my shower.

Then I saw his razor and had a moment of panic that he'd done something crazy like shave his beard, but then I remembered that he liked to trim up his neck to keep it clean and tidy.

Panic attack prevented, I rushed through the rest of my shower, being sure to keep my casted arm in the air to prevent another visit to the doctor's office today.

Once I was through, I quickly snatched my towel off the rack and walked to the mirror, smiling so fucking wide that I nearly cracked my face when I saw the note written on the glass.

It was written in a dry erase marker that I'd seen on the bar in my kitchen the day before. On it there were eleven words that made me impossibly happier than I'd already been.

You looked beautiful last night and this morning. Love you—Ezra.

Any happier and I just might burst.

This day was going to be perfect…I just knew it.

***

It wasn't perfect. It was god-awful.

What I didn't know was that while I was acting out last night, someone was videotaping me. And that video would be shared all throughout school by the time I arrived that morning.

I underestimated the power of a video, too.

Because by seven thirty, after I finished with the middle school drop off, I was the star of the high school campus—and not in a good way.

I hadn't even made it all the way into school when I was stopped in the hallway by Camryn.

"Oh. My. God," she whispered. "We're on video!"

I frowned. "What?"

She pulled up her phone, and a grainy video of me and Camryn was on the screen, showing us rolling around on the mat with my head pressed to her breasts.

Moments after that, we separated, and I got on the bull.

The only reason I knew it was me was the bright goddamn blue cast.

I looked at the offending object and thanked God that I'd gotten it changed last night due to having some beer spill on it while at the bar.

Now the only thing on it was '*I love Ezra,*' who'd signed it this morning on his way out the door.

I hadn't even been aware that it'd been there until a middle school student that I'd helped out of the car started to giggle and pointed it out.

I'd grinned my stupid grin all the rest of the morning drop-off…until right now.

"Son of a bitch," I whispered. "What the fuck?"

Camryn shook her head. "It's too grainy to pinpoint either one of us. As of right now, it's just speculation that it's a teacher at all. I just wanted to warn you."

The warning was a good thing, because I was able to more or less prepare myself when I was called into the principal's office for the second time that week during my conference period.

I walked in like I owned the place and acted like I had no idea why I was there.

"Did I get another complaint lodged against me?" I asked, real worry in my voice.

Though not for the complaint, but for the video.

She didn't know that, though.

Mrs. Sherpa's lips twisted into a grimace. "No, I'm sorry. Quite the opposite in fact. Have you seen the video going around the school today?"

I blinked innocently at her.

"Ummm," I hesitated. "No. What video? Is it of a fight?"

Oh, God. I was so going to hell.

Lying to the principal!

What had gotten into me?

"I have to say, Ms. Crusie, I'm quite disappointed in seeing this video," Mrs. Sherpa noted. "I would've never expected these actions from you."

I widened my eyes and stared at the grainy video yet again, frowning.

"What is it?" I asked.

Really, you couldn't see a damn thing. All you could see were two women lying on the mat and hear them laughing. That was it.

Hell, I could make out Ezra's back better than I could make out my face.

"It's a video of two teachers at the bar 'Ride 'Em Joe's.' The one with the electric bull at it," she explained.

I waited for her to go further into detail, but she didn't, waiting for me to confess, I assumed.

I wouldn't be.

She'd have to prove me guilty without me doing her any favors.

"I don't see the problem," I said honestly. "What is that video of?"

Oh, God. Could she tell that I was lying? My face felt like it was on fire. Absolutely burning up to a crisp. Any moment she'd call me on my lies. I just knew it.

Plus, without validation from the party in the video, she only had speculation and heresy.

Plus, my cast was entirely different than the woman's in the photo.

Luckily you couldn't see Moira's largely-scrawled name on the cast due to the angle the video had been taken from.

"You should be more careful about what you do when you're out in public."

"That's not me," I lied. "And, even if it was me, from what I can tell, there's nothing in that video that's *wrong*."

I hoped there wasn't any more to the video than what I'd seen, because otherwise I'd just totally lied to the principal!

Mrs. Sherpa pursed her lips and then shook her head before placing the phone down on the desk in front of her. "I can't prove that it was you, and I do agree. However, some parents have already called and said that they didn't like how the teachers in this video represented themselves. How they're supposed to be role models for their students…blah, blah, blah. Just pay attention when you're…out."

I nodded.

"And, just to give you an update on the grievance filed against you, we've deemed that it was irrelevant, and if you want your class back, you can have it. However, that being said, I'd suggest letting Coach McDuff finish it for you. If you still want the class next year, it's yours."

I didn't know what to say to that.

I wasn't sure that I wanted it so much as I wanted to finish what I'd started.

"Can I let you know by the end of the day?" I asked hopefully.

She nodded, then stood. "Coach McDuff informed me that you and he are seeing each other."

I bit my lip, then nodded.

"There's no policy on dating between teachers, just make sure that you use discretion." She gave me a wink. "And congrats. I always had a feeling that you and him were going to end up with each other."

My mouth fell open. "You did?"

She nodded. "It didn't escape my notice—or anybody's really— that you had a thing for him. Not in high school, and not now. It's only escaped his notice, I think."

I snorted. "Yeah, I agree. Sometimes I want to smack him for how little he noticed me in high school. It's like this Ezra and that Ezra—the one that he was before he actually 'saw' me—are two totally different people."

She grinned. "Sometimes it happens like that, darling. Now, get to class before you're late."

I did get to class, hurrying down the hall to get to my room before the tardy bell rang.

I would've made it, too, had I not stopped and stared at the way Coach Casper and Ezra were carrying on in the middle of the hallway outside the gym entrance.

I'd stopped and stared, and then growled when I saw Coach Casper put her hand on Ezra's arm, smoothing it up and down as if she wanted to do more than just touch.

I suddenly saw red.

Crossing my arms over my chest, I waited for him to notice me.

I don't know how long it was—possibly an entire minute—before he noticed me, but by the time he did, I was already on plan five of plotting his possible demise.

He suddenly jerked his head up, saw me standing there, and grinned.

Coach Casper turned around to see what he was looking at and scowled.

I would've flipped her off had I not just had the discussion with Mrs. Sherpa about my possible behavior.

Instead, I turned on my heels after offering him a solid 'I'll kill you' glare, and then sped off to my class.

I was almost there, pulling the door closed behind me when my belt loop was caught from behind.

I turned and glared over my shoulder.

I knew exactly who it would be, but my heart still gave a little flip at seeing those beautiful eyes and that smug freakin' bearded face so close to my own.

"What do you want?" I hissed at him.

He grinned. "I wanted to say hi."

I didn't believe him.

Not for one second.

"Hey, Coach Duff," one of the junior varsity players in my class called out. "Is it true that you're seeing Ms. Crusie?"

Coach 'Duff's' hand went around my waist and he pulled me back against him. "Yep."

He popped the 'p' loudly, exaggerating the syllable loud enough that the students started to snicker.

"I heard you were seeing Coach Casper. How can you be with Coach Casper and Ms. Crusie at the same time?" another student, Rebecca, called out.

That was when I felt my stomach sour.

"Sorry, Becky. I'm not seeing anybody else but this hellion in my arms. Could y'all give us two seconds?" Ezra asked as he started to tug me out of the classroom.

"We guess so, Coach Duff!" another student called.

That one I couldn't pinpoint who it was, but I had a feeling it was another one of his junior varsity players. The students that didn't have him as an actual coach called him 'McDuff' while his players called him 'Duff.' It'd been something I'd recognized as I'd spent more and more time with the man.

The door closed in my face, and I sighed and turned, plastering my back against it. "Yes?"

I was still kind of pissed, but I was losing my ire rather quickly since he'd followed me, left Coach Casper, and then declared himself in front of my first period class.

By noon that'd be all over, that was for sure. Once lunchtime hit, there wouldn't be a student in the entire school that didn't know.

"Can I help you?" I asked, trying to hide my non-irritation when he only continued to stare at me with those all too knowing eyes. "I do have a class to teach."

"Summer is almost here, woman." He laughed. "You don't have to teach shit."

He did have a point. The only thing I really had to do with my class was go over the study guide I'd handed out yesterday, and make sure that they didn't have any questions. Which, they likely wouldn't. This was my smart bunch. My all A class that rarely ever needed anything from me other than to run their tests through the automatic scanner.

Now, if this had been my third period class, they'd be pounding at the door already asking for me to check their study guides.

"Whatever," I muttered. "Seriously, what do you want?"

Ezra grinned.

Then he did the one thing I hadn't expected.

He kissed me.

And my entire class behind me squealed—even the boys.

Ezra, laughing, left me there to deal with the havoc he'd created and sauntered down the hallway toward what I assumed was his office.

"That wasn't nice, Mr. McDuff," I called out to his back.

"It's Coach McDuff, Ms. Crusie. Get it right." He winked at me, then turned the corner to the hallway and disappeared.

My high lasted all of thirty minutes.

Why? Because one of my little turd-burglar students had posted a picture of Ezra giving me mouth to mouth, and I was reprimanded by Mrs. Sherpa to 'keep it professional' in front of students in a rather lengthy email.

I just knew that Ezra hadn't gotten one, either.

My suspicions were confirmed when I texted him during the time between third period and lunch.

I was right.

He hadn't gotten one.

But Coach Casper's smug face, the first person I'd seen when I walked into the teacher workroom to grab my lunch, didn't help.

"I hear that you were caught fraternizing," she said stiltedly. "That's quite unprofessional of you, isn't it?"

I spilled balsamic dressing on my white shirt moments after that and then had to count to ten to keep myself from punching her in the nose.

It was Coach Casper giving me a mocking look that had what good mood Ezra had left me with disintegrating.

She'd sneered at me. "I just don't know what he sees in you, but when he comes to his senses and comes crawling back, I'll be here."

"Crawling back?" I asked woodenly.

I didn't want to know.

I didn't want to know.

I should leave before she answered.

I didn't leave, though.

Which proved to be part of my own stupidity.

I just couldn't help myself, though.

I had to know what she was talking about.

Had. To.

"You didn't know?" She snickered. "Ezra and I were a thing before you came along, tripping in front of him and giving yourself a bloody nose. That morning he'd spent the day in my bed."

And that was the straw that broke the camel's back.

Carefully picking up my Tupperware bowl that still had half of my salad in it, I tucked it gently into my lunch box and started out the door.

It was Coach Casper's laugh that echoed through my brain all the way to Ezra's office.

Ezra was busy when I entered his office.

He had on a pair of reading glasses I'd never seen him wear before, and he was talking on the phone to someone while discussing a play that had become illegal between the upcoming season and the last.

He saw me and frowned when he got a good look at my face.

"I gotta go," he said into the receiver. "I'll give you a call back tomorrow once I get more info on the rule. Right. Bye."

Once he hung the phone up, he stood and started toward me, but I stopped him before he could get too close by holding my hand up.

"Stop," I ordered, sounding sad.

He did, tilting his head to look at me.

"What's wrong?"

I crossed my arms over my chest and tried not to scream at him.

But I had to know if it was true.

For some reason, it was extremely important to know whether he'd slept with her or not.

All this time, he'd been with me, but he'd at one time been with her.

"Coach Casper just told me that you and her slept with each other," I said carefully, keeping an eye on his face.

Ezra blinked and then swallowed. "Yes. Before we were an item, I was with her a few times."

And that was my heart shattering on his stupid shit brown concrete floor as it fell straight from my chest.

"You..." I looked down at my hands. "That's...really shitty."

Ezra stood up and started walking toward me, but I held up a hand and ordered him to stop. "No, don't."

He stopped, but not as far away as I would've liked at that moment in time.

I felt my insides quivering as I tried to think through what I wanted to say.

"Do you know what it feels like to be invisible?" I asked softly.

Ezra frowned. "What are you..."

"Because I do," I continued, talking over him. "I know what it feels like, because I fought tooth and nail for you to see me since the first time I saw your face, and you *never saw me*."

His eyes wide, he remained silent, and I suppose he was processing my words.

"You probably have no idea what it's like because you've always been popular. Always gotten exactly what you wanted," I murmured. "You've never been on the outside looking in. You've never sat there and wondered whether or not someone you had feelings for was going to look at you today, make eye contact and smile. I lived for those days, Ezra." I paused. "And you never even knew how much they meant to me until right now, did you?"

"No," he admitted, his voice soft.

I was glad that he didn't lie.

I think it would've been worse if he'd lied.

"The day of my brother's funeral, you said something to me," I told him, my eyes never leaving his. "You smiled at me and told me that I had a bee in my hair. You got it out for me almost as if I was a flower instead of a person. You shooed it away, smiled, and kept walking. You had no clue that you'd just made my day infinitely better."

He cursed lightly. "Raleigh…"

I shook my head. "You dated Chelley and Sheri. Tonya and Megan. Jocelyn and Sonny…"

He placed his hand over my mouth. "Stop."

I shook my head. "All of those others? I could get over. I don't know why knowing that you were with Coach Casper is different…but it is. It burns."

And with that, I left and didn't stop when he called my name.

I didn't have to because just as I'd left his office, I not only noticed that the bell for the next period had rung, but also the entire football team was standing there, looking at me wide-eyed. Oh, and they looked like they'd heard every word.

Incredibly embarrassed now, I rushed out, not looking back.

I was thankful that I only had one period left, and that it was the end of the week to boot meaning I didn't have anything to do after school, so I planned out my night.

And it involved an entire bottle of wine.

***

The icing on the shit cake was the smug goddamn look that Mackie shot me as I walked out of school after letting Ezra know, in no uncertain terms, that he was an ass.

Luckily, I'd told him that while we were in the parking lot—I'd thought away from any listening ears.

Unluckily, as I'd gone to leave, my stupid car once again said that the key fob battery was low, despite having replaced it twice. Meaning that my car didn't start, and I was left stranded. Again.

"Shouldn't you be at practice?" I asked sweetly, forcing myself to stop and talk to him when I wanted nothing to do with the kid that was turning into quite a strong looking man.

A scary, strong looking man at that.

Mackie's lips turned up into a silent snarl. "Coach kicked me out of practice for today because of my 'bad' attitude. Looks like both of us are free...need a ride?"

I snorted. "Negative."

Then I walked down the long driveway that led to the main road in Gun Barrel. Maybe someone I knew would pick me up and I wouldn't have to walk the entire way.

They didn't.

Which gave me plenty of time to realize the error of my ways— and understand that I'd done something stupid by taking my bad day out on Ezra.

***

"Shit," I breathed. "Son of a whore. I've just seriously had a really bad day, Cam. I don't know that I can do..."

"Raleigh." Camryn smacked my thigh. "Ezra loves you. He. Loves. You," she repeated for the fourth time. "Just go tell him you're sorry. You had a bad day, he knows that."

I knew that he knew that.

I still didn't want to go.

I wished I could bury my head in the sand and pretend that today hadn't happened.

I wanted to forget anything and everything that happened before six in the evening last night, or maybe go back in time and tell Camryn that I wasn't going anywhere with her.

"And like I said, it sucks about that Casper chick," she continued. "Everyone hates her guts…but Raleigh, Coach Casper doesn't have Ezra, you do. He can't fix who he was before you, but he can make sure that you're his one and only now. It's time for you to realize that."

Sometimes I loved my best friend, but then again, there were times that I really hated her.

I hated that she was right, too.

Apologies were a bitch.

I'd been a bitch, too, so I guess it was kind of fitting that I had to do something that caused me so much discomfort.

I'd been rude and mean to the man that loved me—that had openly told me he loved me in front of half the student body population— and I was kicking myself over it.

"Fine," I said, snatching the bottle of wine off the counter. "I'll go…and I'm borrowing your car."

Camryn snorted. "Just make sure that you have it back before morning…or pick me up and take me to my appointment. Whatever you want to do."

I gave her a thumbs up and then headed out the door to apologize.

Unluckily, or luckily depending on how you looked at it, Camryn was only a few streets over from Ezra, meaning I only had to drive a short distance to get to my destination.

I can do this. I can do this.

I chanted that to myself as I sat in the car, waiting for the clock to strike seven in the evening and for him to finally arrive home.

Spotting the bottle of wine on the seat next to me, I decided that maybe a drink would calm me down.

And as I sat there and counted down with the clock, I drank, sip after sip, hoping that it would help me gain some courage.

CHAPTER 18

Barbie sure has a lot of nice things for a woman whose knees don't bend.

-T-shirt

Ezra

I watched her chug half the wine with a wide grin on my face.

Getting out of my truck that I'd been sitting in for ten minutes now while I watched her talk to herself, I slammed the door, closed and locked it with my key fob before walking up to Raleigh's window and tapping on it lightly.

She screamed and would've dropped the bottle, but luckily, she at least had a miniscule amount of hand-eye coordination.

"Ezra!" she yelled. "You scared the shit out of me."

I gestured to the door. "Unlock it and let's get inside."

She either didn't hear me or refused to listen. Whatever the reason, she stayed staring into nothing as she finished off what was left of her wine. It took her an entire minute, and by the time she finished, she started to laugh.

I stepped back as she opened the car door but immediately stepped back forward when she nearly tumbled out of the car.

The only thing that saved her from eating gravel was the fact that she still had her seatbelt on when she decided it was time to get out.

I snorted in disbelief as she flailed there for a second before I pushed her back inside, nabbed the empty glass bottle before it could smash into a hundred tiny pieces, and then unbuckled her.

Once she was free of the confines of her seatbelt, she stood up, her legs wobbly.

"You know," she said, sounding chipper. "I really, really, really love you. Like, I've loved you for my entire life kind of love. I don't think that anyone on this planet could love you more than I do."

I felt something inside of my chest start to ease. It'd been tight since our fight this afternoon.

Hearing her say that she'd been invisible to me had been a solid blow straight to my heart.

The sad thing was that she was right. I hadn't seen her. I had no clue why, either. Then and now, Raleigh Crusie was a beautiful person. Not only outside, but inside as well.

I was kicking myself for being so self-absorbed that I didn't see her, too.

Hell, not only had we gone to high school together, but we'd worked at the same freakin' school for going on five years now. Sure, I'd seen her in passing, in high school as well as professionally, but I hadn't allowed myself to think of her that way.

Not until she'd knocked over eight million rolls of wrapping paper in the middle of Target, gotten a bloody nose from my industrial size box of condoms, and then ran to the bathroom while leaving her phone open to practically a porno book in her Kindle app.

Seriously, swear to God, this woman was made for me, and I never knew it.

Before she could wobble a second time, I had her in my arms, and I was carrying her bridal-style into my place.

Once I had her settled on my couch, I went back outside to make sure her car was locked up, only then realizing that it wasn't her car at all, but Camryn's.

Then I felt doubly bad because I'd seen her car at the school today, and guessed that it was once again acting up on her. And I knew that she'd walked thanks to the attendant at the gas station, as well as the teller at the bank, letting me know that she'd passed by there.

"Fuck me," I grumbled, feeling like the lowest piece of crap on the planet.

Her walking home had meant she'd done it in those heels that she'd worn to school on my request, despite her saying that they were uncomfortable.

"Shit," I continued to complain as I walked back inside my house.

The moment I had the door closed behind me, my eyes were once again on Raleigh, who had slumped on the couch and was now drooling on my sofa cushion.

Smiling at the cuteness that was my woman, I pulled out my phone and took a picture of her, quickly putting it as my background before shoving it back into my pocket and carrying her back up the stairs.

Her practically plain cast caught my eye again, and just like this morning, I had the urge to write on it again.

Snatching the black Sharpie off the counter as I walked past, I headed up the stairs and to my bedroom, where I placed her gently on the bed so I didn't wake her.

Once she was down, I uncapped the marker and started to write on her cast.

It took me thirty minutes, but eventually I finished it, then recapped the marker.

Once I was sure that she was comfortable and pulled the covers up around her shoulders, I went to the bathroom and took a quick shower.

When I came back out, it was to find her sprawled out on her belly.

Her socks had been kicked off, and she was no longer wearing her pants.

Grinning, I walked over to where she was laying and ran one finger down the length of her thigh. From her ass cheek where her panties ended to the top of her calf.

She stirred and flipped over to her back, her eyes opening lazily. Then she started to stretch, her arms going up high over her head as she got her entire body into it.

"Hey," she said huskily, smiling.

Then she opened her arms and held them out, indicating with a wiggle of her fingers that she wanted me in her arms.

I went.

What did I look like, I was stupid? I wasn't dumb by any means.

Her face was soft and sleepy as I dropped my mouth down onto her upturned lips.

"I love you, Raleigh," I told her once I came back up for air. "I had a fling with her, but she wasn't for me. You are. It may have taken me a long time to see you, but once you were there, I'll never be able to look away. Not ever again."

Raleigh sniffled, then pulled me in so tight that she temporarily cut off oxygen to my head.

I laughed and rolled with her until she was on top of me, pulling her so that her groin was level with mine.

Then planted both of my hands on each plump ass cheek, pulling her down so that her pubic bone pressed into my ever-growing erection.

Anytime I was around this woman, drunk, scared, sad, horny, or hell, even pissed off as all get out, I wanted her.

The tears. The clumsiness. The anger. None of it scared me away.

I wanted her. I wanted everything that came with having her.

Forever.

My mouth pressed against her shoulder blade, then skimmed up the length of her neck as far as I could reach with how she was lying on top of me. Then I moved it back down, this time using my tongue.

She blew out a shaky breath, then turned so that her face was turned toward me.

"You make me feel things," she said to me, her breath that still smelled like the wine she'd consumed earlier fanning across my face. "Why do you make me feel so many things?"

I snorted, moving my hands up. They went from her ass to her lower back, then even farther to come to rest on her shoulder blades.

"You make me feel a lot of things, too," I admitted. "I love the things you make me feel."

She moved and pressed her lips to mine, her tongue peeking out to lick against my bottom lip.

The move was surprisingly bold for her, and I liked it.

This still buzzed woman in my arms was normally quite willing, but she never actually came very far out of her shell. She was still too shy for that.

One day, I'd get her to tell me the things that she absolutely wanted, but for now, I'd be happy with her drunk self being the more aggressive of the two.

I'd also buy her more wine for the days that I was feeling rather adventurous.

My hands went back down, then immediately back up, this time coming under the clothing that she still had on covering her upper body.

She giggled against my mouth, raising her arms up high over her head for me to get her clothing off easier.

Her bra took less time than the shirt, mostly because I didn't bother taking it all the way off her body. I stopped when it was unsnapped, pushing it up just far enough that I felt her breasts spill out of the cups and press against my bare upper chest.

The droplets of water that were still drying on my skin caused her to shiver.

"Cold," she whispered, running her closed lips over my bearded jaw. "Why didn't you wake me? I would've taken a shower with you."

I would have had she not been so stinkin' cute sleeping.

That, and she seemed like she needed the rest.

She likely hadn't slept well the night before all things considered.

That, and I hadn't allowed her to get much sleep so...

"Because I like to smell you," I told her. "As much as I like the smell of my soap on your skin, I also like the feminine fragrance that clings to you at the end of the day. You smell like willing woman and mine."

She sighed and started to shimmy her hips.

I took that as acceptance to finally allow my hands to slip inside her panties.

Before I could get them to where I wanted them to go, she rolled off of me and started to shimmy them down her legs. Once they were off, she immediately got back to where she was straddling me again, this time completely naked.

She didn't lie against me as she had been doing, though.

Nope, she sat up and leaned over so that her breasts dangled inches from my willing mouth.

I growled and did a partial ab curl, sucking her tit into my mouth and giving it a hard pull.

The hand that had somehow ended up in my hair clenched as pleasure rocketed through her.

Her other hand went to where the towel still lay across my hips and started to pull it free.

I lifted my hips and she partially rose off of me, yanking it free. All the while I kept licking her breast, sucking it and biting it.

"Jesus," she breathed. "The things you do to me."

The things I did to her? What about the things she did to me?

Kind of like right now.

She was pressing that small, soft palm of hers against my length and stroking it. She was unskilled, clumsy, and it felt like the best thing that had ever happened to me.

Her forehead was resting on mine, and the only thing separating us at this point was a thin sheen of sweat that had collected on my body the moment that she came near me.

The woman had the power to bring me to my knees.

"The things you do to me have no comparison," I told her honestly. "You may not like hearing this but…you are the best I've ever had, hands down."

She stiffened.

"And that's because what I feel for you isn't the same as what I felt for other people," I told her bluntly. "You make me want forever."

Her lungs drew in a deep breath, and I could practically feel the questions rushing through her brain.

"I don't have a ring for you yet, because you hit me so hard and fast that I never could've prepared for you," I told her, rolling so that she was underneath me.

Her hands went to my chest, abandoning the soft kneading she was doing to my dick.

She was staring at me like I'd just pulled the proverbial rug out from under her.

"I love you, Raleigh," I told her. "I love you like a quarterback loves the feel of the laces between his fingers. Like a baseball player loves the feel of an old, worn glove that he's put thousands of hours into. Like the goddamn sun and the moon. You're it for me. You'll be my wife one day. You'll have my kids. You'll grow old with me and drink sweet tea on our front porch with me. You'll be mine, and we'll die within a week of each other because neither one of us will be able to stand to be here without the other."

I felt her tears on my lips as I kissed her.

"So that wasn't a marriage proposal?" she teased, her breath hitching slightly.

"No," I told her. "Because I want to do it right. I want to make sure that you have that memory. I want to embarrass the shit out of you and make you tell me yes in front of the entire world. Then I want you to throw yourself at me so hard that we both fall backward, and then get a perfect picture with you dropping your lips to mine."

"You've really thought hard about this," she teased, pushing up so that her lips could run over my jaw.

"I've been thinking about this since the moment I dropped that box of condoms I was buying for my nephew on your face." I bent down and kissed her, letting her feel every single ounce of love that I possessed.

That's when our lovemaking got serious.

Her happy buzz had dissipated over the hours, and no longer was she under the influence of anything but me.

My kisses. My love. My desire.

I let her feel everything that I felt for her and more.

She gasped when my mouth moved to her breast, and one of her legs tightened around me when I went to move down farther.

"No," she denied me, her hands going to my hair. "I want you inside of me. Now."

I would've argued with her had I not had the same urgency currently coursing through me.

I just knew the moment I was inside her, I'd lose control. Hence why I was going to get her off first with my mouth.

But, never let it be said that Raleigh didn't get what she wanted.

It never failed.

She asked, and I'd bend over backward to make sure that she received.

And if she wanted my cock inside her? Well, goddamn, who was I to deny her?

I gritted my teeth and crawled up between her legs, stopping the moment my cock head hit the overheated core of her.

We both hissed—her because my tip had hit her clit—and me because just the feel of her hot, wet, and ready was enough to send everything inside of me jolting into action.

"Shit," I hissed, unable to stop myself.

I had to be inside of her.

Now.

Roughly, I pulled her legs up by gripping the backs of her knees, pushing them out wide once I had her at the right height.

Luckily, my dick decided to find the way without me helping, because as I pushed forward, it automatically notched into the perfect spot—at her entrance—meaning I didn't have to let go of anything. All I had to do was slowly sink inside.

I watched, heart in my throat, as her entrance slowly yielded to my tunneling cock. At first it resisted, still unused to the stretch of my cock filling her despite my having taken her numerous times. But, after pulling out and coating the head in her wetness, I slowly slipped back inside, repeating the process more and more until not a millimeter separated us.

My balls rested against her ass, and my dick was so fuckin' snug inside of her that I was finding it hard to breathe.

"God, you feel so good. Like you were made for me," I panted.

Her eyes were electric, and her breasts were heaving as she tried to breathe through her own arousal.

"I wish we could switch bodies so I could feel…and you could feel," she teased, her hands lifting up to run up and down my pectorals.

My nipples pebbled as her fingers slowly ran over the little discs, causing her to repeat it over and over again.

I felt my balls start to rise and knew that we didn't have much longer.

"One day," I said, pulling out and thrusting back inside. "I'm going to have control when it comes to you."

She laughed and canted her hips, receiving my cock at a different angle, allowing me to go even deeper.

I pushed out her legs even wider and watched, amazed, at how well she took me.

"Play with your clit," I ordered. "This sight is too pretty. I'm not going to make it much longer."

And she did.

But it took her less than three strokes, and then she was coming.

I followed almost instantaneously behind her, the semen in my balls roiling up like an erupting volcano that'd been set to blow for years.

Every single time I took her it was like the first time.

The ripples in her pussy still amazed me. The way her face turned euphoric when she was at the pinnacle of her orgasm drew me in. But it was the way she smiled at me afterward that made me want to stay that way forever.

But eventually we both came down from our highs and my cock started to deflate.

She mirrored my thoughts, though.

"I want to stay this way forever," she whispered.

I growled and took her mouth in a possessive kiss. "When the time comes that I ask, baby? Say yes and we can repeat this every night for the rest of our lives."

CHAPTER 19

The worst part about losing your glasses is that you don't have your glasses to help you find your glasses.

-Raleigh's secret thoughts

Raleigh

I was in such a good mood that nothing, not one single thing, was going to make this day bad for me.

Why was I in such a good mood?

It all centered around a certain sexy football coach that had the power to bring a smile to my face even when I felt like a pile of dog poop.

That morning I'd woken up to a horrible headache that I had nobody but myself to blame, and Ezra's big massive forearm curled around me tight.

It took only moments for memories of the night before to come back to me, and when they did, I felt like I was on top of the moon.

Until I felt the distinct wetness between my thighs that had nothing at all to do with him depositing his release there the night before.

But even then, my period arriving still didn't put me in a bad mood.

With half-closed eyes, I began soaking my panties in Ezra's sink—because hello, I was frugal. I didn't throw panties away even when they deserved to be—I started searching for a toothbrush, finding one quickly in the bottom drawer in a little plastic bag that usually gets sent home when you visit the dentist.

Turning on the shower, I shucked what remained of my clothes and stepped into the spray.

It was blissfully warm, and I nearly moaned as I felt the hot water washing away the smell of sex and other things from the night before.

My hand started to get tired from where I was instinctively holding it up over the spray, so I turned and rested it on the shampoo rack that was toward the back of the shower.

That was when I saw my cast.

Everything inside me froze when I saw all the words that littered the expanse of my arm.

I turned my arm, curling it slightly in, and started to read.

I love you because you're pretty.

I love you because you make me smile.

I love you because you laugh when I make stupid jokes.

I love you when you giggle.

I love you when you snore.

I love you when you drool.

I love you when you're crying and not making any sense.

I love you when you drink a bottle of wine to apologize.

Over and over and over, Ezra listed out why he loved me, and by the time I was finished, I was crying.

My head felt like a million tiny jackhammers breaking it open, but I didn't care.

My shower finished up quickly after that.

I located an emergency tampon out of my purse that I'd thought ahead to bring with me, and then, naked, I lurched for the door.

Opening the bathroom door, I hiccupped slightly as I headed back for his bed.

Still slightly wet, I threw myself at him and giggled through my tears as he yelped when my cold hair slapped against his chest.

"Jesus H Christ," he hissed, trying to move away from the cold.

I desperately tried to move my hair away from him as I peppered his face with kisses. I didn't even care that his breath smelled like the bottom of my shoe. This man, with his stinky breath and sleepy eyes, was all mine.

"God, but I love you, Ezra McDuff."

***

Though my day should've been amazing, everything took a turn for the worse during fourth period, and it all centered around one person.

Morgan.

As if Morgan hadn't suffered enough in his short life, he'd been hit by a drunk driver the night before, and nobody had even realized it until fourth period when the school had called to see why he wasn't at any of his classes.

That wasn't like Morgan at all, hence the reason I'd urged the school secretary to give his mother a call to find out where he was, and if he could get to the school by three in the afternoon to make up his test with me.

Though even if he failed the test he'd still pass, but the kid was on the path to making straight As and I didn't want him to drop that grade any.

I'd just handed out my class's test, and was setting a timer on my desk when there was a knock on my door.

"All right, class," I said, looking over the students, pausing when yet again Morgan's no-show surprised me. "Time starts now. You have fifty minutes."

Everyone turned their tests over at once and got right to work. Giddy with excitement that summer was right around the corner, I walked to the door with a smile on my face.

That smile widened exponentially when I saw Ezra on the other side.

"Hey!" I called, walking out and closing the door behind me.

I reached for his hand and gave it a squeeze, but he didn't squeeze it back.

My smile slowly fell as I got a good look at his face.

"What is it?" I asked, worried now.

He swallowed, and I watched his Adam's apple bob with the movement.

"Jan's gonna watch your class for a minute, come with me?" he asked.

I looked over at Jan, the school's secretary that worked in the front office, and nodded. "Sure."

We slipped by each other seamlessly, and I fell into step beside Ezra.

He didn't say a word until we were in the staff breakroom.

"Ezra, what is it?" I asked, worried beyond belief at this point.

He pulled me until I was in his arms, and then he dropped the worst kind of bombshell on me ever.

"Morgan was hit by a drunk driver last night on his way home from a party. The friend, a kid from another school, is dead, and Morgan is in critical condition in the ICU."

I closed my eyes and started to cry. "No."

***

Morgan had been pronounced dead four times over the last forty-eight hours.

"He's going to make it," I said, so sure that I wasn't the least bit worried. "He's going to pull through. This is just another detour that he has to take, but he's going to get out of that bed. I know it."

Ezra wrapped his hand around my neck and pulled me to him. "I know, baby."

I felt like something was sitting on my chest, and I wasn't sure how easy it would be to breathe if I took a step out of his embrace. For this reason, I stayed where I was and prayed that I was right. That Morgan really was going to live.

"They said that it was a young kid driving a black truck."

We both looked up to find Ezra's nephew standing there. "A big black one that is jacked up with big tires and has green stars on his wheels."

I frowned. "Do you know him?"

Johnson's eyes stayed locked on his uncle's.

That's when I felt Ezra's body stiffen as he said, "Mackie has a truck just like that."

"Really?"

Ezra nodded.

"Really."

"Well then, call the sheriff and tell him!" I urged.

So Ezra did, but unfortunately, Mackie had a solid alibi and not a single dent on his pretty truck.

Who was his alibi, you ask? Coach Casper.

But the timing was off, the suspicion was there, and everyone was watching.

I should've known then that there was something uncomfortably wrong with that picture, but I didn't.

CHAPTER 20

Why is it called 'throat punch Thursday?' Why can't it be 'I can throat punch you no matter what day of the week it is' day?

-Raleigh to Ezra

Raleigh

Four and a half months later

"How was Morgan?" Ezra asked as he walked in the door to my place—our place.

Ezra had officially moved in last week, and we were now living together like one very happy couple.

"Morgan's up, moving around, and complaining that he's ready to get out of the rehab part of the hospital and get home. He says it's not any better than the actual hospital was." I laughed. "It was good to see him smiling."

Ezra groaned and fell onto the couch face first. "That's good to hear. I wanted to go see him, but I didn't find time before visiting hours were up."

We'd done a lot of visiting with Morgan over the last couple of weeks.

Since both Ezra and I had a lot of time on our hands thanks to school letting out, we'd used it to our advantage.

How had we done that?

By moving in together, visiting Morgan, and starting various football and baseball camps for kids of all ages.

Well, I didn't participate in the football camps. I participated by offering my moral support from the sidelines where I sat under an umbrella in my fancy zero-gravity chair with a cooler of cold Dr. Peppers and munchies.

But I was there, and available to help if I was needed—which ended up being a whole lot more than I thought was needed.

"How was work?" I teased.

Ezra rolled over onto his back.

"After you left you mean?" he questioned.

I nodded. "It reached a hundred and four, and the athletic trainer called practice until the rain cooled it down ten degrees. But then it was so humid it felt like we were in a sauna, and *I* called practice because I had sweat dripping down my balls."

I giggled and walked to the kitchen, snatching my phone from the countertop.

"Do you still want to go on a date?" I teased.

He'd promised me that today would be the day that we celebrated our eight-month anniversary—and not the anniversary of us becoming an official couple since we couldn't actually remember—but when he dropped a box of condoms on my face and finally noticed me.

He'd found the receipt for his wrapping paper when we were moving, and today was officially *the* day.

"Sure," Ezra yawned broadly. "I just gotta go take a shower."

I glanced at him.

He was now leaning against the couch with his head buried between two couch cushions—oh, and his eyes weren't open.

"Do you want to try that new place on High Road?" I asked about Poison Jacks, the newest bar/pub in town.

Ezra squinted at me for all of two point five seconds before shaking his head. "Nah. That doesn't look like my type of place."

I walked over to the back of the couch and leaned my hands on the cushions before leaning over so that our faces were lined up, though upside down.

He blinked open his eyes, and I felt my heart flutter in my chest.

"How about a movie?" I asked softly. "We can rent one on Amazon, and I can order pizza."

His smile was soft. "Why are you so good to me?"

I bent until our lips were touching, delicately placing a single chaste kiss on his lips before pulling away. "Because I love you, Coach McDuff. Even when you smell like sweaty balls."

Before I could so much as pull away, he had me around the waist and I was flying head over heels onto the couch.

My shriek of surprise had me shaking as laughter started to pour out of me.

Then, I got an up close and personal interaction with his crotch, and he most definitely didn't smell like sweaty balls. He smelled like sexy man.

And before I knew it, neither one of us was thinking about much of anything but each other.

An hour later, we did indeed end up having pizza and watching a movie, which I guess worked out for us since tomorrow was our first official day back at school.

Ezra had technically been there for the last two weeks when he'd started two-a-days with the football team, but tomorrow would be our first day back as we got our classrooms ready for students.

"I'm not looking forward to tomorrow," I groaned into his side. "I want to live like this forever."

He ran his palm up my hip and settled it just underneath my breasts. "Maybe next year."

I frowned and rolled until my head was resting on his thigh. "Why next year?"

His grin was slow but wide. "Because next year, you'll be my wife, and I hope to have you knocked up before we're home from our honeymoon."

My brows rose. "You have to actually ask me for me to be your wife."

Ezra's eyes flicked back up to the screen. "Are you coming to my CrossFit class in the morning, or do you want me to let you sleep?"

I rolled my eyes.

Ezra and CrossFit.

Ezra had a new love affair with the class. And I'm not talking about 'oh, CrossFit is awesome!' I'm talking, 'if I don't do CrossFit, I might very well die.'

One of his students had urged him to go with him, and that was all it took. He was hooked. He'd started CrossFit at the beginning of the summer, and now, right before the start of the school year, he was planning how to continue doing it with his school schedule.

At first, I'd gone with him purely out of curiosity.

Now, I knew better than to think that CrossFit was for me. It wasn't a joke, and honestly, I'd rather just stick to my occasional walk around the neighborhood.

After dropping a fifteen-pound wall ball on my face instead of catching it, and trailing blood all over the gym on the way to the bathroom like a murder victim, I'd come to the conclusion that things were just better when I didn't participate in extreme sports.

But then he'd made me go a second time…and let's just say that hadn't been the best idea ever.

***

One month ago

"Come on," Ezra urged. "Tomorrow is a partner WOD."

I blinked. "What's a WOD?"

"Workout of day," he explained the acronym as if it was perfectly normal to shorten everything one was saying so that normal, non-CrossFitters, didn't understand half of what was being said. "And I promise, I would not make you come to this if it was hard."

I thought about my bloody nose this morning and cringed. "I'll go if you don't make me go to that same class time. Everybody in there has already messaged me on Facebook asking how my face is. I don't think I could handle seeing them again so soon. At least if I go to a different class, they might think that you abuse me instead of me abusing myself."

Ezra rolled his eyes to the ceiling. "Seriously? You'd rather someone think that I beat you instead of them thinking that you're a clumsy person?"

My laugh was my answer as I'd gone to bed that night, and now, staring at the workout on the whiteboard, I wondered what I'd gotten myself in to.

"Who is Diane?" I wondered aloud.

"Diane is the name of the workout," Ezra murmured, his arms crossed over his chest as he listened to the coach explain what we'd be doing today.

"We're going to do..." That's about when I zoned out. The sheer amount of work he was wanting me to do was flabbergasting.

"You want me to do handstand push-ups?" I asked in surprise.

He looked at me like I was cute—the coach, not Ezra. Ezra looked at me like I was his.

"Yes," the coach, who also happened to be the school resource officer, said. "Honestly, I'd like you to give the handstand push-ups at least a try. I don't expect you to do them all. Heck, I don't expect you to do any. But how will you know if you can even do one if you don't at least try?"

That was true.

I wouldn't know if I didn't try.

But...I had a feeling that I wouldn't be able to do it. I could barely bend over and shave my legs without getting out of breath. How did he expect me to do a handstand push-up?

"You're adorable," Flint laughed. "I swear, I can see every emotion cross over your face. I like you, girl."

The coach was the biggest man I'd ever seen. He was a tanned-skinned hottie that had a buzzed head, a bright white smile, and eyes the color of warm chocolate. I swear he and Ezra had a love affair going when I wasn't around.

Ezra talked about him constantly, and vice versa. Flint had been to a few practices, helping the kids with strength training, and we'd even gone out to eat with Flint and his flavor of the month.

Apparently, this gym was a family to them, and that family included hanging out with them outside of gym hours.

How Ezra was supposed to find time was beyond me. He had two-a-day practices coming up, baseball and football camps, and let's not forget about the fact that he still had to eat at some point in there.

That was truly why I'd decided to go with him.

He didn't like leaving me for his only free two hours a day that we didn't spend either eating, taking a shower, or doing other things that didn't include sleeping when we were in bed.

There really wasn't enough time in the day for all that Ezra had on his plate.

I could see why he didn't want to teach his sex-ed class last year—and wouldn't be doing it this year, either.

Speaking of the sex-ed class, the harassment charge that had been filed against me had gone away just as fast as it'd come. After speaking with some of the students, they'd all cleared my name and said that there was never anything that went on in that class that was inappropriate.

Meaning if I wanted, I could take my sex-ed class back over next year.

I knew that I could.

It all boiled down to whether Ezra would allow me to.

He was so protective of me, and always cognizant of my fears.

Those fears had slowly been put to rest over the summer as I spent more and more time with some big boys on the football team and during the camps. I wouldn't say that I'd be completely comfortable being in a room with his football players, but I'd definitely be open to the idea of one day doing it—which, a long time ago, wouldn't have even crossed my mind.

Ezra poked me on the ass, and I blinked and looked up. "What?"

"You ready?"

Was I ready? Ready for what?

"Sure," I shrugged. "Just don't kill me, okay?"

He didn't have to kill me. I nearly killed myself.

Turns out, I was right about the handstand push-ups. I found out when Ezra helped me do the handstand, and then let me go.

I started to go down into the push-up when my legs started to travel sideways.

My finally out of the cast arm started to give out on me, and I fell.

My face smashed into the mat, my arm went awkwardly to one side. My legs went in a different direction.

Oh, and let's not forget that the wall I was leaning against had a rack of wall balls—one of which had hit me in the face yesterday— against it.

My feet hit the bottom of the rack, and after all that embarrassing stuff with having my face meet the mat, the wall balls added the final insult and finished me off.

Oh, and they got it all on video.

***

"I'll come to your CrossFit class if you take me out to get donuts afterward," I bargained.

"We don't have time to get donuts," he countered. "How about you get the donuts before the class. You can eat them in the corner like the little piggy you are."

My mouth fell open in affront, and I gasped. "You did not just call me a piggy!"

It was actually kind of funny, not that I'd be telling him that.

"If it walks like a donut, and talks like a donut…"

I launched myself at him, and he made an oomph sound as my body hit his. He might've had a chance to catch me had he not been laughing so hard at the look on my face.

"I cannot believe you just said that!" I cried, punching him in the arm repeatedly.

He caught me before I could connect a third time, rolling me so that I was smooshed into the couch cushions and his body was pinning me in place.

I wiggled, trying to break free, and he pushed himself down harder.

"It's okay," he muttered, his mouth only inches from mine. "I like the way you smell when you eat the donuts. And licking the glaze off your lips is about as exciting as it gets for me when I've given up all carbs."

Did I forget to mention, on top of him working his ass off all day long, he'd also given up one of God's greatest creations—carbs?

"I bet each flake of glaze is like two whole carbs," I joked. "You better stay away from me until I can go change my shirt." I pushed my hands up underneath of us and cupped the girls—which had gotten bigger over the last couple of months as I took up his carb intake. It seemed the fitter he got, the fatter I seemed to get.

Though, to be honest, I wasn't too upset on where the fat was going—to my ass and boobs.

Those had always been lacking.

He growled and ground his hips against me, his eyes now on my chest instead of my face.

"I can't fuckin' wait to marry you," he informed me.

My brows rose. "You'd have to ask first, darlin'."

I'd say yes. I'd say yes a million, gazillion times.

Yet, he always alluded to asking, and never straight up asked.

I always got the 'I'm going to do it when you're not expecting it.' And at this point, I wasn't expecting a single thing from him. He was all talk and no action, my man.

Well, kind of.

His eyes were on my tits now, and I could feel an impressive erection pressing against the inside of one of my thighs.

My heart, which always took off at the look that I could now see on his face that meant I was about to be busy, had taken off into unsafe levels.

Yet, I didn't say a word.

Not when he was staring at me like I was the next best thing to the brownies he'd given up a month and a half ago.

"Do you love me more than brownies?" I asked him.

His eyes lifted, and they were hooded and hot.

"You know I do," he answered simply.

"What about Dr. Peppers?" I wondered, a small smirk kicking up the corner of my lip.

His eyes narrowed on that smirk. "More than Dr. Pepper."

"What about those little kolache thingies you used to get at the gas station?" I teased.

He growled low in his throat. "You are about to get your ass spanked."

I was really pushing all of his buttons here.

Ezra was what you could call hangry. All the damn time.

So not only had he given up sugar, but he'd given up bread, noodles and rice.

He was on a low carb, low calorie diet that was really doing impressive things to his physique.

Unfortunately, I couldn't be strong like him.

I now had to sneak food into the house.

Last week, I'd had food in my purse when I was visiting Morgan, and Ezra had walked in during a surprise lunchtime visit to see me with a pile of the no-no foods in my lap.

I'd acted like they were Morgan's and had thrust them at him.

Morgan had laughed at me while he'd eaten them in front of me, and that was when I knew that he was going to be just fine—well, as fine as a boy with limited mobility in his legs would ever be.

Ezra moved and started to run his lips up the length of my neck, pausing at the base to suckle lightly on my collarbone. "You're not paying attention to me."

I bit my lip and moved my hands away from my breasts, running them up his body to curve around his shoulders. "You weren't being very interesting I guess. Don't worry, you have my full attention now."

His chuckle had my insides turning to mush.

"What is it about you that makes me so goddamn happy?" he wondered.

I didn't know.

I couldn't tell him what it was about him that attracted me to him all those years ago, or why it was that I loved him so much. There were just too many things to count.

But I'd give it a try.

"I love you because you're selfless," I said softly, my hands going up to cup his bearded cheeks. "I love that you take time out of your summer to spend with kids—all day, every day—for weeks on end. I love that you'll drop anything to go pick up one of your players. I love that you make me smile. I love that you…"

His mouth slammed down on mine, and all of a sudden, he was in a rush to get me naked.

I didn't stop him. In fact, I helped him.

CHAPTER 21

The worst part about online shopping is having to get up and get your card.

-Text from Raleigh to Ezra

Raleigh

The beginning of the school year

"Who do you have in your class?" I heard one of Ezra's assistant coaches ask.

Ezra and Allic, the assistant coach, traded class rosters, and Ezra whistled. "You have Mackie? Fuck, that sucks."

Mackie was back with a vengeance this year.

I could happily kill the English teacher, as well as the science teacher—Camryn, who'd failed him last year.

Out of all of the kids that needed to get the hell out of this school, he was it.

I hated it even more that I somehow knew he was guilty of hurting Morgan, yet he wasn't punished for the crime.

Morgan was back at school and happier than ever.

"All right, children," Mrs. Sherpa sighed, sounding tired. "Two things before I allow y'all to head to your classrooms to get set up."

We all waited, none of us bothering to question what the two things she needed to say were.

She didn't take long in voicing them, which had been why everyone stayed silent.

"I want to have a great year. We did excellent on our state testing scores last year, and I would like to do the same this year..."

My attention shifted away from Mrs. Sherpa to Coach Casper that was sitting on the opposite side of Allic, and I wanted to throat punch her.

She had her hand on Ezra's hand, and she was practically leaning all the way over Allic to accomplish it.

Not that Allic seemed to mind. He was actually grinning as he tried to suck his belly—which wasn't very big to begin with—in so that Coach Casper would have more room.

His eyes were on me, and he was mouthing something that I couldn't quite make out.

I gave him a puzzled look, and he repeated it.

Her boob is in my hand.

My eyes flicked to the hand that Allic had resting in his lap, and I burst out laughing when I saw that Coach Casper's boob was, indeed, in his hand.

I would've dared him to squeeze it had my laughter not garnered Mrs. Sherpa's attention.

"Ms. Crusie, Coach Allic, Coach McDuff," Mrs. Sherpa said, making me glance in her direction. "Is there something you would like to share?"

I looked pointedly at Coach Casper's boob that was still in 'Coach Allic's' hand and shrugged. "We were talking about a funny story that related to the state test."

"Oh, please enlighten me of this funny story," Mrs. Sherpa said.

"It involves bathroom humor," Ezra drawled, clearly noticing when I needed some help.

Mrs. Sherpa snorted. "Young man, I'm a mother of four, a grandmother of fifteen, and a great-grandmother of two. Trust me when I say that I'm more than capable of understanding and tolerating bathroom humor. So please share."

Ezra's eyes met mine, and I had to bite my lip to keep from bursting out laughing.

"I…"

The fire alarm went off before Ezra had to make up some random ass story about state testing and anything to do with the bathroom.

"Everyone remain calm," Mrs. Sherpa said.

Not a single teacher had risen out of their seat.

I looked over at Ezra again. "No freakin' out, Coach Duff."

He flicked my nose with his pointer finger. "What am I going to do with you?"

Allic groaned, and I realized that Coach Casper had finally moved her breast from his hand.

"You're going to just love me," I suggested. "And put up with the rest."

He linked his hand through mine, and then stood up when the alarm continued to go off. "Probably should get out of here, Mrs. Sherpa."

Everybody followed suit, and I was sad to realize that Coach Casper followed close behind us.

God, what I wouldn't give for that woman to take a flying leap off a tall building. Preferably somewhere where I would never have to see or hear from her again.

Just as I had that thought, I tripped on the seat in front of me, catching the toe of my foot on the metal rim, and pitched forward.

Luckily Ezra didn't even break stride as he caught me up in his arms and continued to walk as if he didn't just save me from taking a header into the older than dirt auditorium floor.

"Jesus Christ," Coach Casper muttered underneath her breath. "Drama queen much?"

I tossed a glare over my shoulder at the woman who had come up to Ezra's other side.

"Are y'all going to teacher night tonight at Poison Jacks?" she chattered as she walked along with us.

I gritted my teeth and started up a conversation with Camryn, who'd come up on the other side of me.

She'd arrived late, and Coach Casper had taken the spot that I'd saved her next to Coach Allic. Coach Allic, who had a major crush on my best friend and could barely speak when she was near.

It was honestly quite cute and made me feel bad that Camryn only had feelings for my brother—feelings that my brother most assuredly didn't return.

"Hey, did you get assigned a new room like she said you might?" Camryn asked.

Thankful for the break in having to listen to Coach Casper's annoying voice, I chattered with Ezra and Camryn as we made our way out the auditorium door.

The moment we were outside, I started for the usual area that my class was assigned to go to during emergency drills but came to a standstill when Ezra came to a bone-jarring halt—me being forced to stop as well or risk losing a limb since my hand was still in his.

"What are you doing?" I asked, confused.

That was when Ezra stopped and curved his arm around my neck, pulling me into his chest.

Camryn came to stand on my other side before Coach Casper could insinuate herself into the spot, and I was thankful that my best friend knew me so well.

"Coach Casper said that Poison Jacks was really good. Do you want to go?"

I could've happily killed Ezra in that moment.

It hadn't escaped my knowledge that that woman was poisoning everything I'd worked so hard to achieve.

Not only was she after Ezra—a man that I'd had my eye on for so long that it should be weird how much I adored him—but she was now after not only my job but my life.

I couldn't prove it, but I felt like something was off.

She was the sweetest person she could be when other people were around, but the moment that you only had Coach Casper—aka Crazy Cunt—she turned into the antichrist.

Seriously, there wasn't a single redeeming quality about the woman that I could find.

"You did not just say that to me," I growled.

Ezra's brows went up. "I didn't say that?"

"Ezra," I breathed in and out deeply, trying to calm myself. "I freakin' asked you to go there, and you goddamn said that it didn't look like 'your kind of place.'"

Ezra's face cleared. "You said it was some pirate place."

"It is," I snapped, seconds away from losing my temper. "It's a goddamn pirate-themed restaurant…called *POISON GODDAMN JACKS!*"

I visibly saw Ezra wince.

"I didn't know that was the place," he admitted.

And before I could smack him upside the head, he dropped down to his knee and wrapped his arms around my waist. "Please forgive me."

I sighed.

I couldn't stay mad at this man for long.

"Whatever."

There was possibly a smile breaking out over my lips, but I wouldn't admit to it.

"Now get up before you embarrass me."

His eyes started to gleam.

"Why would you be embarrassed?" he questioned.

"Hey, Coach!"

I turned to see the football team on the field, having evacuated from the field house while we'd exited the auditorium.

Johnson tossed something at Ezra, who caught it with ease.

I looked back at Ezra and answered him while I shook my head.

"Because when you're down there, you look like you're about to prop…" I trailed off when Ezra palmed the black box that Johnson had just tossed at him.

"Like I'm about to propose?" he asked, flipping the box open.

Inwardly I was screaming my ass off. Outwardly, I was speechless.

"Raleigh Crusie, will you marry me?"

I blinked. "I…"

"You'll…"

"I'll…"

He rolled his eyes.

Camryn punched me in the kidney.

"Say yes, dumbass," she hissed behind me.

How could I say anything but yes?

"Fuck yes!" I cried out, throwing my arms around his neck and tackling him to the ground.

"Language!" Mrs. Sherpa cried out, sounding amused regardless.

"We should recruit her for the JV coaching staff. She just tackled him better than any of the ninth graders I've seen all week," Allic suggested.

I was too busy kissing Ezra to care.

"Can I put the ring on you now?" he asked between kisses.

Blindly, I reached my hand up without once disengaging my mouth from his.

"All better now?" he asked, his eyes shining with mirth. "Does it make you feel better that you're soon going to be mine and everyone will know it?"

I didn't even have to think about it.

"Oh, yes."

But when I finally peeled myself off of him to admire my ring, a dark feeling stole over me when I caught the hostility in Coach Casper's eyes.

Where everyone else was smiling…she was quite effectively pissed.

Ruh-roh.

CHAPTER 22

Do you ever feel like your body's check engine light is on and you're still driving it like 'nah, it'll be okay?'

-Text from Raleigh to Camryn

Ezra

With one final thrust, I buried myself to the hilt and came so hard that if I wasn't already laying down, I would've fallen.

"Jesus Christ," I growled, pushing and pulling my cock in now, loving the way her pussy rippled with aftershocks of her own orgasm.

"So much better than going to CrossFit with you," she murmured. "Soooooo much."

I chuckled and pulled out, loving the wet sound that it made when we separated.

Reaching for the towel I'd just used to dry my body off with, I pressed it against her now-leaking core and got up off the bed, glancing worriedly at the time.

"Shit," I groaned, walking to the closet. "I'm so late."

Her husky laugh behind me had me contemplating hopping back in bed with her and going for round two, but I was already running late as it was, and the coach wasn't allowed to be late for practice when he was required and paid to be there.

"Love you, Ez-E," Raleigh called, getting herself more comfortable in the sprawled position she was already in. "And don't let that woman hang on you. I hate her."

I snorted.

That'd been her parting shot every morning since I'd proposed to her.

Out of everything that had happened that day, she was still stuck on the fact that I'd asked her if she wanted to go to Poison Jacks.

"She won't," I promised.

"That's what you say every time, and when I walk around the corner, she's running her hand up and down your arm."

That was true. Coach Casper was a toucher when she spoke.

"I'll do my best," I paused with my shirt halfway over my head. "How about that?"

"I guess that's good enough." She rolled and settled onto her side. "Will you turn out the light already? I still have an hour until I have to get up."

I chuckled and fished out my tennis shoes, a clean pair of underwear, and my socks out of my dark closet.

Once I had them all, I took them to the bathroom and closed the door, getting dressed in there.

Moments later, fully dressed with deodorant on, I flicked off the light and hurried toward the bed.

I kissed my woman goodbye and started to walk out the door when Raleigh's words stopped me in my tracks.

"Coach Casper really does worry me," she whispered.

I swiveled on a heel and turned to stare at her through the darkness.

I was on my way to the practice, and I didn't really have time to spare. Not when I spent thirty minutes of the forty I usually used to shower and change after my early morning workout making love to my soon-to-be wife.

"I know," I murmured. "But I can handle her. Just know that I love you and that you're the woman I'm going to marry."

Raleigh relented. "Yes, Coach."

Grinning, I left the house and hurried to my truck, jumping inside and starting it up before I even had the door all the way closed.

Moments after that, I was backing out of the driveway and hurrying toward the school.

I was going to be late, so I called Allic and asked him to get started on a few drills without me until I could get there.

He agreed, and by the time I arrived at the school I was already six minutes late.

Coach Casper's car was parked at the front of the lot where the staff was allowed to park, and I had to wonder why she was here this early when she didn't have practice until the afternoon.

Giving Raleigh's parting words a whirl, I contemplated heading straight for the field.

Knowing my assistant coach was on the ball unlike me, I made a detour to my office to grab a couple of protein bars since I hadn't had a chance to grab breakfast after my workout today.

Only, when I got to the hallway that led to my office, a sound alerted me to someone using it, causing me to freeze.

"Oh, fuck." I heard a low, breathy moan. "Yes, harder, baby."

My brows rose, and my mouth dropped open in surprise.

Someone was having sex in my office!

Somebody was using my office as a goddamn bedroom, and I was pissed.

When I pushed the closed door open moments after inserting my key into the lock, I wasn't prepared for what I found.

Nothing could've ever prepared me to see Coach Jacklyn Casper and Mackie Tombs fucking on my goddamn desk—both of them completely buck ass naked.

Mackie was pumping away while Coach Casper got her fill— literally and figuratively—and not paying the least bit of attention to me or the now not-so-empty office.

I backed away slowly, and stood beside the door, wondering at what I should do.

My first inclination was to snap a picture to ensure that I was believed, but in the end, I decided to go down the hall to the trainer's office and pull him in. Only, instead of finding the trainer, I found the school resource officer.

Flint Stone was in one of the trainer's rehab chairs reading something out of a file folder.

He looked up when I entered.

"Problem, Coach?" he asked, looking concerned.

"Uhh," I hesitated. "I need you to witness something."

Flint was a good man. He was a thirty-three-year-old vet and had a damn good head on his shoulders. I liked him and respected him a lot, so I knew that he could handle what was about to happen.

"This isn't gonna be pretty," I told him right before I led him to my office, where the fucking had gotten more exuberant.

I rounded the corner at almost the same instant that Flint did and was unsurprised when his 'holy fuck' left his mouth, causing both Mackie and Coach Casper to gasp in surprise.

"What the fuck?" Flint boomed, using his Marine voice.

If I wasn't so goddamn flabbergasted about what was going on in my office, I might've asked the same goddamned thing. Sadly, I was not just surprised, but pissed, causing me to momentarily question everything that was about to come out of my mouth.

"Get dressed," I ordered Mackie. "Coach Casper…clothes."

Then we turned around as I dialed Principal Sherpa's number.

Moments after that, I called the cops.

I was sick to my stomach.

The two had crossed quite a few moral boundaries.

And all I could think about the entire time that I was sorting shit out for the next hour was that Raleigh was right…and she was going to freak the fuck out.

***

The moment that our eyes met, I knew that she knew.

Her eyes were rimmed with darkness, and she looked tired.

I was sure that she'd been woken up by the gossip mill. If not by another teacher, then by the students.

The football players had figured out rather quickly what had gone on when a couple of police cruisers had shown up, taking both Mackie and Coach Casper to the police station. From that moment on, the players had let their mouths run like wildfire, spreading the news far and wide.

The moment she came within a foot of me, I pulled her into my arms, causing the students in the hallway around us to all go, "Awwww."

I rolled my eyes and pulled Raleigh into my classroom that I used for the next three periods, looking at her with wide eyes.

"Well, I hear that you got a little action today," she whispered teasingly.

I rolled my eyes. "I wish I didn't. I can't erase that shit from my brain."

She patted me on the hand and then leaned in so that the front of her body was pressed to mine.

"Makes me wonder about other things, too," she murmured.

"What other things?" I questioned.

"Other things like Coach Casper being Mackie's alibi for that night that Morgan was hurt."

It sickened me to think about it, but the more I thought on it, the more likely it became.

I should've said something then about it, but before I could, the bell rang and Morgan himself rolled into my class with a wide smile on his face.

"Can I be the ring boy at your wedding, Coach?" he called as he passed. "I'm about the same height as one."

I rolled my eyes. "Sure, Morgan. Whatever you want to do."

With that my woman patted me on the cheek and told me she would see me later, and I momentarily forgot that there was something I wanted to call the chief of police about until too late.

CHAPTER 23

Peezing- sneezing and peeing at the same time.

-Text from Raleigh to Ezra

Raleigh

My stomach was roiling, and the only thing I could do was sit on the couch and look at Ezra and his niece pitifully.

"No, listen." Moira shook her head. "It's not going to come! I know. It's my face!"

Ezra shook his head. "Listen, Snaggletooth. It's going to come out, I promise. I know these things."

Moira shook her head. "No, you listen, Coach Duff. You're not pulling it out."

"What if I pull it out really fast?" he offered.

The little girl didn't even take the time to consider his offer.

Moira shook her head. "Your hands are too fat. I came over here hoping that Aunt Raleigh could get it out with her small fingers. Not your fat ones."

I bit my lip and tried not to laugh, knowing if I did it'd make my stomach hurt worse.

I had a bad case of food poisoning.

Ezra had a touch himself, but he hadn't eaten the full portion like I had. He'd only had a tiny little bite.

Thank God.

Otherwise we'd have both been sharing the one single bathroom while we both did things out of both ends that should never be shared amongst a couple—at least not this soon in a relationship.

Today, however, we were babysitting, and I was lying on the couch that Ezra and I spent our first date on.

I hadn't contemplated moving in well over four hours.

Every time I did, the food poisoning would come back with a vengeance.

"Well, *Aunt* Raleigh," he drawled, looking over at me with a bemused smile, "can't do it right now. You'll have to either let me do it or come back later."

She sighed. "Fine. You can do it, but if you screw up, it's on you."

Ezra snorted and held his hand out for the paper towel.

"Why isn't your mommy doing this again?" he asked teasingly.

Moira gave a long, dragged out sigh. "Because Mommy cries when I cry."

"You're going to cry?" Ezra started to look worried.

Ezra was a sweet man. What was even sweeter was his love for his niece.

Moira had all the men in her life wrapped around her pinky finger, and that was no exaggeration.

If Moira cried, Ezra would be sad.

This should be fun.

"Maybe," Moira offered. "But if I cry, just keep going. It's gonna happen."

"Okay," Ezra said worriedly. "I'll try to accomplish that."

Moira had really grown up over the last couple of months. Her vocabulary had sky-rocketed as kindergarteners were bound to do. It was awesome seeing her excel.

Speaking of language...

"Okay, pull!" Moira ordered.

Ezra tried.

He really did.

But when he tried to pull, he couldn't get a good grip on it and ended up also gripping the small tooth beside it.

Then the little girl screamed, and big crocodile tears started to roll down her cheeks.

Ezra freaked.

Literally freaked.

"Oh, God." He dropped the towel, which had a smidge of blood on it. "Are you okay?"

"You hurt me, Uncle Ezra!" Moira cried.

I couldn't help it.

I laughed.

"You think this is funny?" Ezra turned and glared at me.

Yeah, yeah I did.

"Moira," I said softly, pitifully. "Come here and let me try."

I went up to my elbow, and once I was able to hold my throw up down—thank God—I went even farther up to my butt.

I felt drained and completely blah, but I managed to get myself upright and hold my hand out for the paper towel.

"My turn," I said softly.

Moira picked up the towel and ran toward me, holding it out while she continued to cry.

I didn't waste time on the tears. Instead, I gestured to the couch and said, "Come sit. Let's get this done."

Because I might very well need to throw up again, and I don't want to throw up in front of you.

"Okay," Moira sniffled.

I bit my lip to keep the smile from my lips and positioned myself.

"That one?" I asked, wiggling it to test its readiness.

"Uh-huh," Moira mouthed. "'At one."

Hooking my fingernail around the back of the tooth, I pulled.

Moira screamed—but not the scream of pain, more the scream of surprise—and then the tooth was out.

Ezra glared at me. "I loosened it."

I snorted. "No, you fell for the crocodile tears."

Ezra shrugged. "I fall for yours, too."

That was true.

I smiled weakly.

"I don't cry to get you to give me things, though," I admitted. "I cry because I'm a klutz that can't keep herself upright."

Moira took the tooth I held out to her in her hand, and then ran out of the room without so much as a thank you.

Once the door slammed, another wave of nausea hit me.

That quick, I ran for the door, all thoughts of teeth and Ezra's smile forgotten.

***

It was the phone call that woke me from a dead sleep.

"Hello?" Ezra growled.

I rolled over and stared at Ezra's back. I could barely make him out, and the only thing in the entire room that was lit up was the alarm clock that read '3:03' and the light from his phone.

"Gotcha," Ezra assented as he stood up and made his way to the closet. "Don't let them leave. I'll be there in ten minutes, max."

With that, he hung up and blew out a long breath.

"What is it?" I muttered into his pillow.

I was so tired. After the afternoon we'd spent watching Ezra's niece while his sister took her son to the doctor in Dallas, I was not happy to find the phone ringing in the middle of the night.

The nausea had finally abated, but I could still feel traces of the food poisoning causing my system to abhor the thought of food.

Pairing that with the fact that we'd started school back three days ago, and I was practically a zombie, I was not doing well. Granted, we'd only had the students there for two of them, and it was now officially Saturday morning and I didn't have to do anything tomorrow, but I just couldn't rouse myself long enough to get out of bed and go with him.

"Couple of my players were caught loitering in the school parking lot. I'm heading there to take them home," he murmured.

I moaned. "I'm going to kill them."

I felt his phone hit the bed and blinked one eye open to see him quickly tugging a shirt over his head.

Ezra chuckled and bent over the bed, placing a quick kiss on my cheek. "I'll do it for you on Monday at practice. Don't worry."

With that, he left.

I heard the sound of his truck start up, but even then, I was only conscious long enough to think that his truck was really quite loud at three o'clock in the morning.

It was the ringing of the phone that woke me up again.

This time when I blinked open my eyes, it was to find that the clock read three forty-one.

Son of a bitch.

Reaching blindly for the phone that I now realized Ezra left, I snatched it up and placed it to my ear, muttering a 'hello' that likely didn't sound as coherent as I'd meant it.

"Got a kid of yours here, Coach," I heard. "He's drunk off his ass."

I blinked open my eyes and stared hard at the wall in frustration. "Where is here?" I asked. "And this is the coach's soon-to-be wife."

He rattled off the address. "Sorry if I woke you. I normally call the coach when his kids are in trouble."

I brushed off his apology and sat up, heading for clothes that had been hastily discarded onto the floor when we'd arrived home. "I'll be there in ten. Don't let him leave."

He should've let him leave.

Why?

Because it wasn't a player of Ezra's that was drunk off his ass. It was an ex-player of Ezra's, and the kid that scared the bejesus out of me.

Before I could tell him to find his own ride home, he climbed in my car and I had a choice to make.

It was the wrong one.

***

Ezra

I pulled into the driveway and stared at Raleigh's missing car, a sense of foreboding overtaking me.

The moment I got inside, I searched for the phone that I'd left on the bed and found it amongst the hastily cast-aside sheets.

After looking up the last number to call, I groaned and headed back out to my truck.

As I went, I made the call back to Chocchie.

"Yellow?" he answered, sounding tired.

"Chocchie," I said. "It's McDuff. You got my girl there?"

Chocchie grunted. "She just arrived to pick up your boy."

"Which one?" I asked, already heading back out to my truck.

"The one with the smart mouth," Chocchie said as if that was enough for me to figure out who it was. Didn't he know that they all had smart mouths as kids?

"That doesn't really narrow it down, man," I grumbled, getting into the vehicle and starting it back up.

"Hold on," he paused. "I'll go...oh, fuck me. Shit, shit! Call 9-1-1!"

I didn't know who he was talking to, but by the time I arrived at his bar two and a half minutes later, I had a very bad feeling in the pit of my stomach. One that grew when I arrived to find Raleigh on the ground, holding a white bar towel to her face while she watched Chocchie try to keep Mackie on the ground.

When I arrived, I threw the truck into park and bailed out of the truck before I'd barely gotten the damn seatbelt off.

Moments later, I was helping Chocchie pin Mackie to the ground, knowing instinctively that the little shit was responsible for the blood I could see on that white towel over Raleigh's nose.

"Raleigh, call the cops."

Raleigh replied with a shaky, "Already did, baby."

***

"I swear to God, Ezra," Raleigh said in exasperation. "It's only a freakin' nose bleed."

"A nose bleed caused by a six-foot-two person punching you in the face," I said, sounding just as angry as I felt. "Please, humor me."

She sighed and took my hand, wincing slightly when her palm came into contact with mine.

"Hurt?"

She nodded. "Yeah. I think I might have jammed a couple of fingers. Who knew that punching someone in the face would hurt that bad?"

My temper was already stretched to its limit, so I chose not to answer or reply at all as I waited for the doctor to arrive to check Raleigh over.

Lucky for us we had a personal physician that was used to our late-night wake-up calls.

"Do you think they'll give him bond?" Raleigh asked, leaning her head against my shoulder.

I shook my head. "No. Maybe. I don't know. I don't think he wants to go out. Honestly, I think he's exactly where he wants to be since that's where Jacklyn Casper is." I paused. "In a sick sort of way, he knew exactly how to get there to be with her."

"But they don't put men and women prisoners together," she pointed out.

"No," I agreed. "But I don't think Mackie was thinking all that clearly."

Coach Casper had done a fine job on fucking Mackie up, that was for sure.

"Did you hear that he confessed to hitting Morgan?" she whispered. "He said he couldn't drive his truck anymore because it was 'fucked up from hitting that cripple.' That it didn't 'drive' right after they got it fixed so fast. He said that when I got there to pick him up."

That was news to me.

Then again, a lot had gone on from the moment that I'd arrived.

The cops had arrived within two minutes of Raleigh calling 9-1-1, and Mackie had been spouting off a bunch of bullshit while we'd had him pinned to the ground.

A lot of which centered around me ruining his life.

Which, in some ways, I suppose I had.

At least the one he thought he had with Coach Casper.

But that relationship was fucked-up at its finest. I had zero guilt for turning her into the authorities for taking advantage of a student like that. For Mackie to be that fucked, she'd had to have done a doozy of a number on him.

"You were right," I admitted. "There was something wrong with Coach Casper."

She started to laugh, but that laugh quickly turned to a moan.

Then she was running in the direction of the bathroom.

"Maybe you should get the doctor to run a flu test on you as well?" I suggested, watching her heave.

Raleigh moaned into the toilet bowl just as the doctor came into the room. "Please tell me you did not pull me out of bed at four o'clock on a Saturday morning to confirm a pregnancy test."

I froze as pieces of the puzzle finally started clicking into place.

Raleigh threw up again for good measure.

"Actually," I paused. "Raleigh was punched in the face, and she punched someone else in the face in retaliation. We need to get her checked over to make sure she doesn't have a broken face...or possibly a broken hand. The pregnancy thing, though..."

Raleigh threw up again.

"We probably don't need that confirmed until tomorrow."

The doctor chuckled. "Oh, Raleigh dear. You always do keep my life exciting."

I looked over at Raleigh, who was leaning her head against her arm. "She keeps my life exciting, too, that's for sure."

EPILOGUE

*No matter how bad it gets, I'm always rich at the
Dollar Store.*

-Bumper Sticker

Raleigh

"I'll see you tomorrow afternoon, baby," Ezra said in my ear.

It was two in the morning, and Ezra and the team had a long drive ahead of them to where they were playing their next game.

I made a non-committal sound that was somewhere near an 'okay' and a 'narrrhg.'

He laughed quietly and pushed away. "I'll give you a call when we get there."

I gave him a thumb up, and went back to sleep until something woke me up a few hours later.

I listened, ears perked, for the sound that had woken me.

Not the baby.

Otherwise she would've cried out again by now.

I opened my eyes and tried to see the time on the clock but couldn't get my eyes to quite focus long enough to read the letters.

Then a movement of some sort caught my eye, and my eyes moved from the clock on the nightstand to the bed. There was a blob…something glowing in the dark…on the foot of the bed.

I frowned, the haze of sleep making thinking cognitively difficult.

Again, I tried to get my eyes to focus, but I was just so freakin' tired that I was finding it hard to do much of anything besides close them again. Then, whatever it was—the blobby mass that glowed in the dark—moved.

It. Moved.

Logically, I knew that this wasn't a good thing. There shouldn't be anything glowing in the dark and blob-like in my bed.

Unless it was a toy…

I reached out and poked it, my finger going into something extremely squishy and warm.

I pulled back, and tried to produce what might possibly be squishy, warm, blob-like, and glow in the dark.

And couldn't figure out what that would be.

At this point, I decided that maybe whatever it was just might be a figment of my imagination, and I could just ignore it.

So, I did what any sane, rational person would do at that point.

I kicked it off the bed, then rolled over and closed my eyes.

That's about when the piercing screams started.

***

Ezra

I pulled into the parking lot of the ER and found the closest parking spot.

Once the car was in park, I got out and shut the door, beeping the locks with my key fob before jogging into the building.

I arrived and immediately walked up to the cop at the front desk—Atley.

"Hey, Atley," I called out. "Have you seen my wife and kid?"

Atley nodded his head and then gestured for me to follow him.

I did, following him through a maze of hallways until I arrived at a door that was partially closed.

"Thank you, Atley," I said softly.

He nodded his head and continued on to the nurses' station, looking bored.

I would be, too. It was seven in the morning, and the only car in the parking lot had been mine and the staff.

I pushed in through the door and felt my heart melt at what I saw.

Raleigh was sitting up on the exam table, her eyes closed, her head resting on the top of our son's head. He was in his glow in the dark pajamas that I'd dressed him in last night, and his curly blond hair was a rioting mass that went every which way but the one it should.

His little arm was wrapped up tight in an ace bandage, and it was covering the majority of his face as he snoozed away, impervious to the harsh fluorescent lights that were shining bright.

Our daughter was cocooned in the mass, too. I could just make out the fuzzy, brown curly hair peeking out just above the baby carrier that Raleigh had her wrapped up in.

All three of them slept, Raleigh partially reclined on the exam table, the rest of her leaning against the wall at her back.

I found myself breathing deep since I'd gotten the call and pulled out my phone so I could remember this exact occasion.

The shutter of my camera had Raleigh's eyes snapping open, and the moment she saw me, she started to cry.

"I didn't mean to!" she whispered fiercely.

I found myself walking farther into the room and leaning both arms on the padded bench beside her hips. "J never gets into our bed, honey. It's not your fault. You didn't mean to, either."

Her lip quivered. "I didn't know what it was. I honestly thought it was that Build-A-Bear that we bought him last week. The Iron Man thing that glows in the dark?"

The 'Iron Man thing' was actually a Star Wars thing, and she was right. His lightsaber did glow.

When I'd gotten J dressed last night, I'd seen those pajamas hanging up in the closet, and I'd realized that they were almost too small for him and he hadn't even worn them yet. After putting them on him, I'd gotten him into bed and closed the door— unaware that by doing that I'd be putting him in something Raleigh wouldn't recognize in her weakened state.

If anything, I blamed myself for her tiredness, too.

I'd brought the flu home from school, and had given it to her, Charlotte, and J. Raleigh had been the last one to get it, but she didn't have time to lay around miserably. She had to take care of our babies because I was knee deep in football playoffs.

Not that my woman would ever complain.

In the two and a half years that she'd officially been mine, she'd never once not been there for me, and I felt like I'd failed her time and time again. I always put her first…but it never felt like I did— especially during playoffs.

Not that she would ever say that.

It was just how I felt.

"I love you, Raleigh," I told her. "And this is not your fault."

A couple of hours later we were sprung from the ER, and I went back to work, but this time I took my family with me.

I had tried to leave them at home.

Raleigh wouldn't think of it, though. Not with her favorite student shining in the spotlight.

***

A few days later, I stood at the podium and called out Morgan's name.

"Morgan Leigh Bryce, your senior spokesman for this year's graduating class!"

Morgan had changed quite a bit over the last year.

Time had definitely been in his favor.

Though he still was quite literally bound to his wheelchair, he was making great progress.

Morgan rolled his wheelchair—he refused to have a motorized one after the low battery incident where he fell out of his chair—and came to a stop at the steps.

When I realized what he was about to do, I stiffened with pride.

Then he did the unthinkable.

He moved the brakes on the wheelchair in place and then started to stand.

The entire two hundred and eighty-nine students, who knows how many faculty, and parents here gasped in shock as he made it to his own two feet.

Morgan was a good kid, and well liked all around. His accident had rocked our entire community, and there wasn't a single person in the entire room that didn't know his story.

When I saw him stand, my eyes automatically went to my wife in the side row where the faculty had come to witness the senior night.

Morgan and Raleigh had been through a lot over the last couple of years, but the year that I'd met her and made her mine had definitely been the most trying. Raleigh had been there for him when nobody else had thought to look at him twice.

Nobody else would've seen the sadness in his eyes—at least not someone that didn't have that bleakness in their own.

I hadn't realized the extent of both of their anguish until I'd seen them talking out in the hall all those years ago—the day I realized that I wanted to date her. That I wanted her to be mine.

And now, seeing how far that Morgan—and Raleigh—had come made my heart full.

Morgan took his first step up onto the platform, and I heard Raleigh burst into tears.

Consequently, so did Morgan, who turned to her with a smile on his face.

He winked at her, and then turned back around to continue climbing.

It took him a lot less time than I would've expected.

Forty seconds instead of the minutes that I'd seen him do the night before.

Then he was taking slow, measured steps across the podium until he reached me.

I held out my hand the moment he was close enough to reach it, and then shook his before I couldn't stand it anymore.

I threw my arms around him and hugged him hard. "I'm so fuckin' proud of you, kid."

Morgan squeezed me back. "Thanks, Coach."

Then I stepped back to surrender the microphone to Morgan.

When I took a seat at the rear of the stage, I watched, just as everyone else did, as Morgan began his speech.

"You might not have known it, but two and a half years ago, I was well on my way to committing suicide."

There were more inhaled gasps.

Raleigh and I were likely the only ones in the entire place that realized there'd ever been something wrong with the kid.

"I was in a bad place. I didn't like getting up and facing a day where I couldn't walk. I couldn't get into the shower without help, and not a day went by where I didn't think about how much easier it would be on me and everyone else if I wasn't there to need to be taken care of," Morgan continued.

"But then Mrs. McDuff, previously Ms. Crusie, changed my life." Morgan's gaze turned to Raleigh. "She said something to me...told me a joke...and I couldn't figure out why I was laughing, but I was. She said, 'What is a soldier's least favorite month?' and then told me 'Allich.'"

The crowd laughed.

"And I spent the rest of the day thinking about that laugh that she coaxed from me." He looked at my wife, who was still looking really run down.

But, since it was senior night and Morgan was our well-loved water boy, she'd come to support the seniors.

"She didn't know that she saved me," he said, sounding happy. "But she did." He looked back over the crowd. "Mrs. McDuff was that teacher for me. The one that changed my life. The one that parents always hope that their children have. The one that makes sacrifices and spends her own hard-earned money on school supplies. The one that comes to games even though she hates them. The one that will do anything in her power to make sure that you excel in life. And I have a feeling that I won't be the only life that Mrs. McDuff changes."

No. Morgan definitely wasn't the only one that my Raleigh had changed.

She'd changed me.

She'd made me a better person.

She'd been there when I hadn't even realized that I'd needed a person to lean on.

She was the one for me, and always would be.

Hell, she was such a good person that she'd fought for Mackie to be taken to a mental health facility to help him move on with life. To help him see that what he had with Coach Casper was bad.

And as of a few weeks ago when I had checked on him, he'd been doing well.

Not that I particularly cared whether he was or not. But Raleigh did.

As for Coach Casper? Well, she'd lost her teacher's certification, was now a registered sex offender, and was spending about eight years in jail for her crimes.

"I don't think any of us would be here without Mr. and Mrs. McDuff. So thanks to the McDuffs for getting us to where we are today!"

The newest graduating class of Gun Barrel High cheered.

We turned to each other and grinned. Them Morgan gave me a high-five

ABOUT THE AUTHOR

Lani Lynn Vale is married to the love of her life that She met in high school. She fell in love with him because he was wearing baseball pants. Ten years later they have three perfectly crazy children and a cat named Demon who likes to wake her up at ungodly times in the night. They live in the greatest state in the world, Texas. She writes contemporary and romantic suspense, and has a love for all things romance. You can find Lani in front of her computer writing away in her fictional characters' world...that is until her husband and kids demand sustenance in the form of food and drink.

Made in the USA
Middletown, DE
23 September 2024

61383008R00155